Raves For BUST, the First Collaboration From KEN BRUEN and JASON STARR!

"Two of the crime fiction world's brightest talents, Ken Bruen and Jason Starr, join forces for one of the year's most darkly satisfying and electric *noir* novels…This is one of the top guilty pleasures of the year."
— *Chicago Sun-Times*

"This tense, witty, cold-blooded noir…reads seamlessly—and mercilessly…Funny [and] vividly fresh."
— *Entertainment Weekly*

"A full-tilt, rocking homage to noir novels of the 1950s…A seamless blend of Bruen's dead-on Irish underworld and Starr's hellish vision of the Big Apple, Hard Case's latest release is smart, trashy fun."
— *Publishers Weekly, starred review*

"Fasten your seat belts, and enjoy the bumpy ride of double- and triple-crosses, blackmail, and murder. If Quentin Tarantino is looking for another movie project, this novel with its mix of shocking violence and black comedy would be the perfect candidate. Highly recommended as a terrific summer read."
— *Library Journal, starred review*

They called him Slide because he didn't let anything slide, ever. He'd killed thirteen and counting. Counting like the ritual psycho he was. Counting on there being more—lots more. He was, as they say, only getting warmed up.

The name, trademark, signature if you like—that's right, he had a signature—came from what he'd whisper to his victim before administering his coup de grace.

"Know what, partner?...I'm gonna let it slide."

Ah, that sheen of hope, that desperate last dangling moment of reprieve. It got him hot every time.

He had looks to kill, like a wannabe rock star. Long dark hair, falling into his eyes, always the black leather jacket and the shades, knock-off Ray-Bans. He wore a thin band on his left wrist, woven by the tinkers. He didn't come from the classic horrendous background. He was that new comfortable Irish middle class—lots of attitude, smarts and a mouth on him. Raised in Galway, he'd been to the best schools, never wanted for anything. His passion was all things American.

He had one sister, always in his face, taunting him about his long hair, his huge blue eyes that girls would swoon over. They'd been swimming, his sister and him, and literally, in a second, the voice said, "Drown the bitch."

He did. Whispered to her, "Was gonna let it slide."

Maybe the world didn't know it yet, but Slide was gonna be one of the greats. Dahmer, Bundy, Ridgway, Berkowitz, Gacy, and Slide. But he needed cash to finance his dream. Piles of it.

And that was how Slide got into the kidnapping biz...

SLIDE

by **Ken Bruen**
and **Jason Starr**

A HARD CASE CRIME NOVEL

A HARD CASE CRIME BOOK

(HCC-036)

October 2007

Published by

Dorchester Publishing Co., Inc.

200 Madison Avenue

New York, NY 10016

in collaboration with Winterfall LLC

ISBN 0-8439-5776-X

ISBN-13 978-0-8439-5776-1

Cover design by Cooley Design Lab

Typeset by Swordsmith Productions

The name "Hard Case Crime" and the Hard Case Crime logo are trademarks of Winterfall LLC. Hard Case Crime books are selected and edited by Charles Ardai.

Printed in the United States of America

Visit us on the web at *www.HardCaseCrime.com*

For Chynna and Grace
and
For Paul, Eileen, Colleen, and Nicole, the whole gang
at Dead End Books on Long Island
(www.deadendbooks.com)
and
For independent booksellers everywhere,
without whom...

SLIDE

One

*Some people never go crazy. What truly horrible lives
they must live.*
CHARLES BUKOWSKI

Max Fisher opened his eyes, looked at the blurry mess around him, thought, *Where the fuck am I?* He managed to turn his head, stare at a wall. It was a white wall. The walls in his apartment were white—okay, he was probably home. What day was it? He thought it was Monday because yesterday was Sunday, right? Didn't he see a football game on TV, at the bar he was drinking at? Or was that two days ago? Wait, it wasn't football, it was baseball. It was July for Christ's sake. The Fourth was just, what, last week? He remembered loud noises, explosions, fireworks. Yeah, it definitely wasn't football season.

He rolled over toward the night table, misjudged it, fell onto the floor. Right on his hip. Must've been a bad fall because the pain killed even though he was still smashed.

"Aw, Christ," he said, wincing, tasting vomit.

He stayed like that for a long time, might've passed out, then managed to struggle to his knees. The pain in his hip was excruciating, but he figured if he'd broken something he wouldn't be able to move.

Using all his energy, he squinted, trying to focus on the digital clock. There was a 7 there and a 1 and was that a 5? No, it was an 8. 7:18. There was light outside behind the curtains so it was morning—okay, things were coming together. Then he made out the letters above the numbers: W E D S. Fuck, it was Wednesday morning—a workday. He had meetings to go to, people to see, deals to close.

Holding onto the bed, using all his might, he was able to stand. It was hard to stay upright, though. What was with the floor? He needed to shower, put on a suit, get to the fucking office. He took a couple of steps, almost fell, then a voice reminded him, *You don't work anymore.*

Then it all came back to him, how his whole life had been ruined by his former executive assistant—and, briefly, ex-fiancée—that Greek-Irish whore, Angela.

Angela. Max wished he could strike that name from his brain, like they did in that Schwarzenegger movie, *Total*…what the fuck was the name of it? Max couldn't even watch TV anymore. *Angela's Ashes*, Angela Lansbury, Angela Bassett. Suddenly Angelas were fucking everywhere. Even on the street there were reminders— the hair, the tits, the sickening Irish accent. One day Max heard a tourist near Rockefeller Center go to his friend, *I'd fancy a pint me own self,* and Max wanted to strangle the Guinness-loving fuck.

The first time Max had laid eyes on Angela and her incredible bust, he should've known how things would turn out. Big tits meant big trouble; every guy knew that. Max always listened to his instincts, but the one time he let his guard down—kaboom.

Things had been great before she came along all right; yeah, his life had been hopping. He was the fucking man, the head honcho, the big enchilada, you ask anyone. He was a player and he had freaking mega plans, he was riding that gravy train all the way to the goddamn zenith. He owned a successful computer networking company, lived in a spectacular town house on the Upper East Side. Then Angela came along. Fucking Angela. She was like a living curse, a goddamn virus.

And not only had the cunt wreaked havoc all over his perfect life, she'd given him herpes! When you see those blisters in the morning while you're having a long lazy piss, you see agony, you see fucking terror.

After Angela ran off to Ireland—charging the flight on his AmEx—he'd gotten revenge. One night he was drinking at some bar in the Bowery and he met a witch, Glinda. Her name wasn't really Glinda—he didn't know what the hell her name was—but that was what he'd called her in his mind. Anyway, Max went to her, "You mean you can cast spells?"

"Of course I cast spells," she said, as if offended. "I said I'm a witch, didn't I?"

Max glared at her, then said, "Yeah, well, I want you to put the evilest spell you can come up with on my ex-fiancée. Make her life and everybody's life around her a total living hell."

The witch cast the spell, said it was the harshest she'd ever done. Did Max sleep with her afterward?

He vaguely remembered some wild, crazy woman, babbling about Wicca while he was banging her, but that could've been a dream.

The witch's spell might've ruined Angela's life, but it didn't make Max's any better. So Max had been trying to drink Angela out of his mind. It had been working, too. Or at least he'd thought it had been working until he wound up here. Wherever here was. And the sad truth was this wasn't the first time something like this had happened. Blackouts, those holy rollers in twelve-step programs called them. But this was worse than usual. Before now he'd never gotten fucking *lost*.

After stumbling and wobbling into the bathroom, Max looked at a mirror, almost not recognizing the bum with swollen, bloodshot eyes and pasty white skin and strings of greasy gray hair hanging over his face. And why were his teeth all yellow, and was one *missing*?

"Aw, Jeethus," he lisped. Or Jaythus, as that Irish cunt would say. "Not a toof gone. Gimme me a fucking break."

Max's big problem was, despite all he'd been through over the past few months, his ego was all there. He might've looked like a cesspool on the outside, but inside, he was still the same happening, suave, debonair, hip Max Fisher he'd always been.

He splashed some cold water onto his face and toweled off and something clicked. The towels—they weren't his. And the vanity and tiles—this wasn't his bathroom. Where the fuck was he?

He stutter-stepped back into his bedroom. Wait, it wasn't his bedroom, it was a fucking hotel room. He parted the curtains and brightness stung his eyes like he was Dracula getting out of his coffin. His eyes finally adjusted and he saw a parking lot. He was in a motel, on the ground floor.

"Jeethus H," he said.

It took him a while to find his pants on the floor. They had stains all over them. He put them on, inside out first, then the right way.

"Shirt, shirt, hell's my shirt?" he said, fumbling and stumbling around the room.

Finally he found a wife-beater T slung over a chair and put it on.

When he opened the door, the sunshine stung his eyes again. He went to the front of the motel, to the office. A young unshaven blond guy was on the phone.

Max stood there, rolling his eyes, while the guy took forever to get off the phone with his girlfriend or whoever. Max felt like raising hell for this kind of treatment—write letters, make phone calls, get this jackass fired. Firing people, this was Max's gig, how he'd risen to the top. And, by Christ, he'd rise again.

Finally the guy hung up, said, "Can I help you?" and Max went, "Where the fuck am I?"

The kid gave Max a look like he'd never heard the word fuck before, then said, "The Golden Star Motel."

"Where the fuck's that, Jersey?"

Another long look. Max wondered if the guy was retarded, had one of those learning disabilities. Or maybe he was dyslexic, was hearing everything backwards, like he thought Max was speaking Hebrew.

Finally the kid went, "You're not serious are, you?"

"Do I look like I'm not fucking serious? I don't see buildings anywhere so I know I'm not in goddamn Manhattan."

No pause this time, just, "Sir, you're in Robertsdale, Alabama."

Max looked at him like he was full of shit, said, "You're full of shit."

The kid showed him a business card, a brochure. Shit, Alabama. And the kid's accent wasn't Jersey; it had southern hick written all over it. That also explained why he was so slow, like everything Max said seemed to have to bounce off a satellite before reaching his brain. Didn't they fuck sheep or their sisters or both down here?

"How the hell did I get here?"

Long delay then, "Well, according to what it says here on the computer, you checked in yesterday afternoon."

"But how?" Max said. "I live in fucking Manhattan."

The kid didn't have an answer to this, just stared at Max with a stumped expression.

Max said, "So where is…" He squinted at the brochure, holding it arm's length away because he didn't have his reading glasses. "…Robertsdale."

"About forty miles from Mobile, sir."

Jesus, sounded like the name of a freaking Glen Campbell song. And gee, like that really helped. Like the whole world knew fucking *Mobile*.

Baffled, Max returned to his room. He sat on the foot of the bed, racking his brain, trying to piece together the last few days of his life. He didn't make much progress. He remembered seeing that baseball

game on TV at a bar in New York. It was definitely in
New York, he was sure of that. Wasn't it that place
in Hell's Kitchen he'd been drinking at? Yeah, he remembered the bartender, the black guy, trying to cut
him off, telling him he had a drinking problem. Max,
who'd been schmearing the guy for weeks, must've
given him five hundred bucks in tips, said, "Are you
fuckin' kiddin' me?" He realized he wasn't when the
bouncer carried him out of the place, dropping him on
a pile of garbage.

Max had no idea why the bartender wanted to get
rid of him, but the idea that he had a drinking problem
was the biggest joke ever. Max Fisher couldn't handle
his liquor—yeah, right, that was a good one. Max knew
he'd been drinking a lot lately—well, pretty much all
the time—but he knew his limit; he knew when to
stop. He was just in an alcohol phase that's all. He was
de-stressing, doing what he had to do to get by till it
was time to get back in the game. Look at all the big
players in every sport, didn't they all have a time out
for abusing *something*? Fuck, it was almost mandatory.
It was freaking un-American not to have some *issues*.
Dr. Phil built a career on it, for chrissakes. Besides,
Max knew he was in total control and could kick the
habit whenever he wanted to. That was the key.

All this thinking about drinking was making Max
crave one. The few empty bottles of vodka and scotch
strewn on the floor whetted his appetite even more.
He went around the room, going, "Booze, booze, where
the fuck are you? Come out, come out, wherever you
are." He needed the wag of the dog, or whatever the

hell it was called. Finally, under the bed, a bottle of Stoli, one quarter full. To hell with the glass, it tasted best straight from the bottle. Mmm, yeah, like that. Yep, it was hitting home big time. Max Fisher was back, all right.

Re-energized, Max formulated a POA—get to Mobile, fly back to the city, figure out some way to straighten out his life once and for all. But, whoa, big problem: his wallet was on the dresser, but there was no cash, no credit cards. For all he knew, somebody had stolen his identity, was going around New York, pretending to be him.

Max tossed the wallet away, grabbed the bottle of Stoli, muttered, "Welcome to fucking Robertsdale," and went bottoms up. The booze started weaving its dark magic almost instantly—reason you drank the shit, right?—and Max thought, *Okay, you need a plan, Maxie, that's all. One simple plan and get back in that goddamn saddle, let the suckers know Maxie is back. Think, Maxie, think.*

At that moment there was a knock on the door—talk about kismet—and a Mexican woman outside went, "Housekeeping."

Then it came to him out of, like, nowhere. He sat up, energized, muttered, "But have I got the *cojones*?"

The last gulp of Stoli assured him he had.

Two

A hole is nothing at all, but you can break your neck in it.
AUSTIN O'MALLEY

He was one dark, dangerous, lethal motherfucker. No one knew the truth of this better than his own self. They called him Slide because he didn't let anything slide, ever. He'd killed thirteen and counting. Counting like the ritual psycho he was. Counting on there being more—lots more. He was, as they say, only getting warmed up.

The name, trademark, signature if you like—that's right, he had a *signature*—came from what he'd whisper to his victim before administering his *coup de grace*.

"Know what, partner?...I'm gonna let it slide."

Ah, that sheen of hope, that desperate last dangling moment of reprieve. It got him hot every time.

He had looks to kill, like a wannabe rock star. Long dark hair, falling into his eyes, always the black leather jacket and the shades, knock-off Ray-Bans. He wore a thin band on his left wrist, woven by the tinkers. He didn't come from the classic horrendous background. He was that new comfortable Irish middle class—lots of attitude, smarts and a mouth on him. Raised in Galway, he'd been to the best schools, never wanted for anything. His passion was all things American.

He'd adopted a quasi-New York tone, learnt from

movies and TV. His dream was to live in the Big Apple.
Yeah, he actually called it that. His vocabulary was a
blend of John Wayne, *The Sopranos* and De Niro. He
was twelve when he discovered his talent for murder.

He had one sister, always in his face, taunting him
about his long hair, his huge blue eyes that girls would
swoon over. They'd been swimming, his sister and
him, and literally, in a second, the voice said, "Drown
the bitch."

He did. Whispered to her, "Was gonna let it slide."

The rush was near delirious, better than any jerk off
to *Guns and Ammunition*. And fuck, even better, he
made it look like he'd tried to save her. Got all the
kudos that brought.

His father was into hunting, a successful attorney.
Gentry and shooting pheasants, made his dad feel like
a player. Slide shot him in the back. Terrible hunting
accident, shame these things happen.

Slide was suitably traumatized. Yeah, right. Laughing
his arse off as they comforted him. Duped everyone
except for his mother. She knew, maybe had always
known. The morning of Dad's funeral, she confronted
him, said, "You are the devil."

He didn't let that one slide.

Maybe the world didn't know it yet, but Slide was
gonna be one of the greats. Dahmer, Bundy, Ridgway,
Berkowitz, Gacy, and Slide. The only problem with
this killing gig was it didn't bring in any dough. He
couldn't sell his memoirs and film rights till he was
dead, or at least on death row, right? He also knew if
he really wanted to make his mark, he would have to

move to America. In the world of killing, the land of opportunity was the big leagues. It was easier to get guns and ammo and there were lots of people who needed killing. Compared to Ireland, America would be a goddamn playground. But he needed cash to finance his dream. Piles of it.

And that was how Slide got into the kidnapping biz.

It hit him one day that he was great at abducting people. He'd done it plenty, leading up to a murder. But wasting a victim right away was a major, well, waste. He thought, Why not hold onto a few, ask the relatives for some cash, and *then* waste them? Call it his Oprah moment.

To master the art of kidnapping he studied American films like *Ransom, Frantic, Hostage,* and *Don't Say a Word.* He knew the mechanics of abduction, but had trouble on the follow-through. He knew how to do ransom notes and torture his hostages, but having a man or woman bound in his basement was way too tempting, and sometimes instead of collecting ransom, he'd kill them, chop up the bodies in his bathtub then bury them. His backyard was like downtown Baghdad —start digging, you were likely to hit bone somewhere. No one amused him like his own self and once, when his shovel clanked against an old victim, he muttered, *Boner.*

Late one evening he was out in Dublin, searching for a victim, when he saw a woman walking alone along Dawson Street, near the Mystery Inc bookstore. Now come on, was that an omen right there or what? She had acid blond hair, a full figure, kind of reminded him of a few hookers he'd offed. But she was classier than a hooker; you could see that from across the street. A woman like her, some guy would pay a fortune to get back.

The pick-up was usually the tricky part. If you're going to stuff a girl in a car, you had to move fast before she screamed her arse off. Or if you were going to lure her, you had to be clever, pour on the charm. But this woman turned the tables—she came up to him. Rushed up, more like it. Slide was baffled. This had never happened before. All his victims in the past had sensed the danger, the looming moment of truth. But this woman was fearless. Even ol' Ted Bundy would have been confused.

She sized him up, smiled, went, "Hey, I'm Angela, wanna buy me a drink?"

The rest, as they say, was history.

Three

At four in the morning, nobody's right.
THE ODD COUPLE

Angela Petrakos had arrived in Ireland with big dreams, an engagement ring, and ten grand in cash. She also had a gold pin of two hands almost touching. The pin was her lucky charm, or at least it was supposed to be. She wore it everywhere she went, figuring the luck part would have to kick in eventually.

Her first day in Dublin she sold the engagement ring to a pawnshop and blew the proceeds in about a month. Then it was time to piss away the rest of her money. The ten thousand dollars had been Max's "emergency fund," a wad he'd kept hidden, with a roll of duct tape, in a shoebox in his bedroom closet since 9/11. Angela used to go to him, "What's some money gonna do if they, like, drop the bomb?" and Max would come back with, "Who knows? I might have to bribe somebody to drive me out of the city or something." Like he thought he'd simply *drive* through a nuclear wasteland. Had anything that bollix said ever made any sense? Had she really agreed to marry him? What the hell had she been thinking?

At first she stayed in the Clarence Hotel on the Quays in Dublin, and jeez, did that Liffey stink or what?

The hotel was owned by U2, but had she seen Bono, or the Edge, or even a fucking roadie? Had she fuck.

When she'd arrived her money had seemed like plenty to get started with but hey, no one told her about this strong Euro. When she'd changed her Franklins, she couldn't believe how it translated, almost cut her nest egg in half. And cash wasn't her only problem. She'd been born in Ireland but raised in the States. In America, her accent was always recognized as Irish and a definite plus. Here they heard her as a Yank and kept busting her chops about Iraq. Like she sent the troops in. She didn't even know where the shithole was.

One day she returned to her room and discovered her key card was no longer working. Beautiful, right? Bono was canceling world debt but not, it seemed, hotel bills. Leaving the hotel, down in the zero, she fingered the pin in her lapel. It was like a prayer she almost believed.

She needed more Euro and she wasn't about to go looking for a job. After a string of bad jobs in America she'd had it with working. Besides, the demand for office assistants who typed twenty words a minute wasn't exactly staggering. A man had always been her first step to money, to getting on track. *Get a guy, get centered* was her motto. The fact that men had fucked her over each and every time had slipped her mind.

She walked along Ormond Quay, passed the very fashionable Morrison Hotel. Unfortunately she didn't have enough to buy a goddamn coffee in there. She continued, her hopes sinking as she watched the area take an Irish dive. Then she hit the fleabags, where the 'non-nationals" were housed, and found the River Inn. It reminded her of some of the shitholes she'd seen on the Bowery and the Lower East Side.

The guy behind the desk snarled, "Money up front, no visitors in the rooms and…" The motherfooker gave her the look, sneered, added, "No clients in the rooms unless you want to pay extra."

She was mortified, like the scumbag was calling her a hooker.

She roared, "You'll get yours, you bastard."

He would, but not in any way Angela could possibly have foreseen.

Angela's room was shite, simple as that. When she turned on the light, the roaches scattered, as if they didn't want to be there either. Cum stains on the bed-spread—God only knew what the sheets looked like—crusted snot on the pillow cases, dirty towels thrown on the floor, and a turd floating in the toilet. Jaysus, good thing she wasn't planning to spend very long—maybe, if her prayers were answered, not even a single night. Dressed to kill, in fuck-me heels, the micro skirt and the sheer black hose, she set out to score.

She went to Davy Byrnes on Duke Street. Her *Lonely Planet* guide—and fuck they got that right, she was as lonely as a banshee without a wail—said it was the watering hole for the yuppies, the moneyed young whizzers. Mott the Hoople's "All the Young Dudes" had unspooled in her head when she read that.

Well, the place had men all right—older men. Okay, she could do old, long as they had the moolah.

Guy in his fifties hit on her right away, said he was

an accountant. His name was Michael. He was bald.
He was barely five feet tall. But, most importantly, he
owned lots of stock and property—including a place in
the South of France—and, the clincher, he drove a
Merc. Want to find a good man, find out what kind
of car they drive. Michael gave her some shite about
James Joyce drinking at Davy Byrnes. She thought,
God, is that his line? She thought she'd heard them all,
but a guy trying to win her over with Joyce was a brand
new experience. Over the next year, she'd be hard
pressed to enter a pub that Joyce hadn't rested his
elbow on. She'd sometimes wonder, when did he get
the time to write all them impossible-to-read books? If
he was drinking that much, no wonder the writing was
so incomprehensible. And another thing, everyone in
Ireland bored the ass offa her about him but no one
had seemed to have actually read him. They'd seen the
Angelica Huston movie and that was the whole of their
Joyce expertise. Go figure.

She moved in with Michael pronto at his flat in
Foxrock. No zip codes in Ireland, probably because
the wild bastards couldn't count. They uttered some
neighborhoods in hushed tones, with the appendage
Dublin 4, and that was enough.

Foxrock was most definitely Dublin 4 and Michael
was lovely, as the Irish say, for a while. He took her out
for nice posh meals, bought her silk lingerie from Ann
Summers, Dublin's version of Victoria's Secret. Course,
being a man, he bought stuff he liked that no woman
would ever wear. She brought it all back, got the cash,
building towards a nest egg. Good thing. Like so many

times before, with so many other guys, he turned. Once they'd screwed you, once you were, as Irish men so delicately put it, well shagged, they lost interest. Michael's personality turned too. Where was the accountant who'd seemed like an Irish version of Jason Alexander? All the weak bollix had ever hit was the books and now, now he was walloping her! The silver-tongued devil.

One night, after watching *What's Love Got To Do With It?* and listening to Nancy Sinatra, Angela felt empowered and took off. Went right to an ATM and withdrew as much of Michael's cash as she could. Angela's rule: before you let a guy ride you, you get his account details. In his case, it was easy. The code for his ATM was JOYCE. She couldn't make this shit up.

It was back to the River Inn and the sneer of the gobshite at the desk. So began a year of hell, the search for Mr. Right. There were ups and downs—mostly downs. Men supported her for a while, seemed to truly like her, but there was always a flip side. Married men told her they were single just to get laid, under-age guys told her they were eighteen. One night, she was date-raped by a lawyer. Angela managed to get to the bathroom, grab a can of Lysol, and spray it into the cunt's eyes, but she was starting to see a disturbing pattern here. She was a magnet for trouble. She was seriously thinking about packing it in, going to play for the other team. She wasn't attracted to women, but she wasn't attracted to a lot of the guys she was sleeping with either. Besides, it seemed like every guy she got involved with wound up hurting her. And it wasn't just emotional pain. No, these men were leaving visible scars.

Self-help books were no help. *Richard and Judy*— fuck 'em. Even a talk with a shrink didn't do crap. She didn't go into formal therapy, but one night she started talking to a woman who was staying in the room next door to her. The woman mentioned she was a counselor and Angela invited her to a pub for a drink. When Angela started to describe some of her experiences with men, the woman started checking her watch, suddenly announced she had "an appointment." Angela never saw the woman again.

Soon afterward, she hit rock bottom. It was her thirtieth birthday. Her clock was ticking. She didn't have many eggs and she knew she'd be a great mother, she knew she had so much to give. It was back in the fishnet hose, back to pumps, back to the same old same old.

After a night of fending off the usual losers, she headed back to the hotel. She was wondering if it was all worth it and was considering a life of celibacy. Was it too late to become a nun?

Then she saw him, watching her from across the street. It was Bono. Well, close enough anyway. He had the rock star gig going on full force, with the hair, the sunglasses. Not Bono-style glasses—they looked like knockoff Ray-Bans—but, hey.

She was tired of waiting for guys to come up to her, being so fucking passive. Didn't the psychology books say she had to assert herself? So when she saw him staring at her, she thought, Who the fook cares any-more, and went up to him, and said, "Hi, I'm Angela, want to buy me a drink?"

The line worked like magic. Better yet, she could tell he had a good soul, that she'd found the real thing. Had it always been this easy?

He offered to skip the drink part and go right back to his place. Angela wasn't opposed. With a ticking clock, you had to move fast. Hell, if he asked her to marry her in the morning she'd say yes. As long as he was decent in bed, was willing to support her and her children, what did she have to lose?

There were a few things early on that caught her attention. He drove a Toyota. No Merc but, hey, it wasn't a mini either. She noticed a strange odor in the car, like he'd washed it with ammonia. On the dash-board was a St. Bridget's Cross, and when she asked him where the name Slide came from, he said, "From the Old Irish." She wasn't sure what this meant, but she figured, he was a religious guy—good sign. Then again, the micks, they'd kill you for a five spot and confess in the morning.

They went to a small house—more like a cabin—on the outskirts of the city, some place named Swords.

When they entered, Angela went, "Ted Kaczynski live here?" but for some reason the joke fell flat. Okay, so maybe he didn't have a sense of humor and he wasn't much of a talker either, but he was still cute as hell. She was dying to be kissed or—who was she kidding?—humped. If this didn't lead to a relationship, at least she'd get a good lay. She hadn't gotten any in over a month and when Angela Petrakos wasn't getting any, look out world.

His place was, if not dirty, in need of a woman's touch, that was for sure. There were beer cans on the couch, garbage on the coffee table. Then she saw rope and chains, which got her hopes up—maybe he was into kinky sex? But when she asked him about it, he muttered, "Haulage business," and changed the subject, going, "Sorry me flat is such a wreck."

She didn't want to tell him that she was *way* into the whole chain thing. At this early stage, she didn't want to make him think she was *that* kind of girl or anything. Much later, she'd learn all about restraints, the kidnapping, but not yet.

There was more painful silence as she watched him go around, cleaning the place.

Then she asked, "Do you read Joyce?" figuring she'd get that nonsense out of the way fast.

He gave her the look, the same one he gave her when they met on the street. His eyes had, what? A shine? A light? No, more like a fevered intensity. She liked them…a lot.

He said, "I've done Joyce, but I prefer non-fiction, *mi amor*. You familiar with *The Road Less Traveled*?"

What was with the Italian and was he trying to talk with a New York accent? He must've been trying to impress her, because she'd lived in New York. He was so cute, the pet.

Liking him more and more—which usually meant

there was trouble ahead and lots of it—she asked, "You haven't ever been an accountant, have you?"

After a rich, warm-the-cockles-of-yer-heart laugh, he said, "Baby, the one accounting I do is off the books."

She laughed her own self. Christ on a bike, how long since she'd done that? A year? Not since New York, and even then there wasn't exactly a lot to laugh about.

He got a turf fire going, gave the room a nice glow, and then they began to fool around a bit. Nothing heavy, the guy wasn't all over her. He was tender almost. Then he made some hot toddies, even added cloves, saying, "Cloves, cos, I'm like the devil, baby."

Things heated up. They got naked and he said, "Turn around for me." Like an order, but she was into it. Then he took her fiercely and abruptly and she came with a scream.

Lying alongside her afterward, not even breathing heavy, he asked, "You know I was planning to kidnap you, right?"

Angela, playing along, still nearly breathless, gasped, "Kidnap me anytime you want, baby."

Four

I grabbed her thin wrist, jerking her onto the bed. I was more than brutal, savage really; I didn't even go through the preliminary of kissing the dumbfounded girl.
CHARLES WILLEFORD, *The Woman Chaser*

Max's big plan: mug the chambermaid, use her five bucks to ride the Greyhound outa this shithole.

The maid knocked again, went, *"Hola,"* and Max was ready to rock 'n' roll. He stuck his hand under his wife-beater like a concealed gun, opened the door, and went, *"Hola* right back atcha, sweetheart." Then he took a closer look, saw a young smiling pregnant girl holding a stack of towels, and he couldn't go through with it. What was he gonna do, roll some knocked-up Spanish broad for her last *pesetas*? What kind of guy was he? Okay, okay, he was desperate, but come on.

He took the hand out of his shirt, said, "Sorry, señorita, it was just a joke, *Avril* fools," and slammed the door in her face.

What the fuck was he gonna do now? He still needed a way out of this mess. If he had to spend any more time in Alabama his brain would start to erode, he'd become as stupid as that kid at the desk. Next thing, he'd be eyeing sheep.

Okay, he thought, *Who can I call? Who can bail me out?*

He couldn't think of a single name and, at some point, passed out.

When he woke up, his head was splitting, felt like it was falling off. Then, he realized that was because it *was* falling off. Well, off the bed anyway. Not really, but he was lying on his back, with his head at the foot of the bed, his mouth sagging, like he was doing a backwards, upside-down blow job scene in a porn movie.

He called his bank in New York. He was surprised to find out he only had $632 to his name. How the hell'd that happen? He thought he'd had two grand last time he checked. He arranged to have money wired but since it was Saturday and because he was no longer a preferred client—what the fuck?—he would have to wait until Monday morning before the money arrived.

This was crazy—how would he survive two more days in Robertsdale? He needed food and more booze, not necessarily in that order.

He left the room, headed back to the motel's office. The sun was as bright as car headlights shining directly in his face. Did the sun, like, ever set in the south?

The blond kid at the desk was on the phone again. Max had to wait till he was off, but this time he had to be polite about it—after all, the kid could be his meal ticket.

When the kid ended the call, Max offered his widest, most congenial smile, and said, "I have a bit of a… um…er…um…problem."

Max let the smile linger and then realized the kid

was looking at him in a weird way. Max was clueless for a few seconds, wondering if staring was another side effect of the kid's mental disorder, and then realized it was because of the missing tooth.

"Oh, yeah," Max said. "Cap fell out last night. Fucking dentist. When I get back to the city, his ass is so fired."

Max continued smiling.

The kid went, "So how can I help you, sir?"

Southerners, they were so goddamn polite. You can stick a knife in a guy's back and he'd go, *Thank you, sir. Have a good day now, hear?*

"Yeah, well, I seem to've, um, er, lost my wallet. Not my wallet itself—I still have that five-dollar piece of shit. I'm talking about what was inside it—the cash, credit cards. You know, my money."

"Sorry to hear that, sir."

Sure he was.

"So I was just curious," Max said, "did I happen to leave a credit card with y'all at the desk?"

That was the way, slip in "y'alls" and Southern-speak whenever possible. Max wanted to show the kid that deep down, despite all their differences—like level of intellect, etcetera—they were one and the same.

"No, actually, sir, you're all paid up."

What the fuck? Max never, ever paid for anything in advance. He almost shit himself—literally. He cut a nasty booze-fart then asked, "What?"

"The Chinese guy paid for your room, up front in cash, sir."

The kid was smiling, like he knew. But knew what?

"Chinese guy?" Max said. "What Chinese guy?"

"He seemed like a friend of yours. He had his arm around you."

The kid gave another knowing, smirking look.

Max remembered, when he'd woken up, feeling some pain in his rectum. He'd thought, *hemorrhoids*? But was it possible that....

Oh, God, Max didn't even want to go there. If this wasn't a wake-up call he didn't know what was. From now on, no more mixing Scotch and vodka. He had to draw a line somewhere, right? And didn't Chinese, like, wear off fast? Five minutes later, you wanted more? Holy shit.

"Whatever, whatever," Max said. "So the room's paid through the weekend, right?"

"No, actually, sir, you were supposed to check out today. The Chinese guy—that's right, said his name was Bruce. Yeah, he took off early this morning."

Max was thinking, *Bruce!* Fuck, if that wasn't a gay name, what was? Wait, Bruce Lee wasn't gay. He'd had a kid anyway. And Bruce and Demi had had a whole litter, hadn't they? There was still hope.

"Look, here's the bottom line," Max said. "I don't have any money, and I won't have any money till Monday morning. So what I need you to do is front me."

"Sir, we can't—"

"Look at me, kid. Understand who you're dealing with. I'm Maximilian Fisher. I'm a man of wealth and fame."

The kid looked confused. Shit, the missing tooth,

the dirty wife-beater, and the farting wasn't helping Max's cause.

Max went, "You're not superficial, are you…sorry, what's your name?"

"Kyle," the kid said. "My mom and dad, they were big *Twin Peaks* fans."

Not in the mood to hear the kid's life story, Max said, "Okay, okay Kyle…Look, what I need y'all to do right now is look beyond what you see in front of you. Ignore appearances, ignore perceptions." Max realized he was using big words; he had to dumb it down, keep it to one or two syllables, or the kid would get confused. Max went, "Just because I don't look rich, don't mean I ain't." Shit, that was too dumb. He didn't want to offend the moron. Bringing the level of conversation back up, Max said, "Look, Kyle, I've dabbled in Buddhism, okay? I'm not a monk or anything like that, but I meditate, get into myself, you know? And what I've learned from my studies, I mean the bottom line of all of it, is that the real world is bullshit, it doesn't even exist. What really exists is what doesn't exist at all—the inner self. So let's talk to each other, one inner self to the other here and—"

"Sorry, Mr. Fisher, I can't front you on the room."

Fuck Buddhism. Max wanted to strangle the dumb hick.

"You have Web access at this shithole?" Max asked.

"Yep, we sure do," Kyle said, "but—"

"Lemme show you a thing or two," Max said.

Max got behind the desk and went online. Although his company, NetWorld, had gone belly-up, the Website was still live. When Kyle saw the picture of Max sitting on the red Porsche with the two D-cup blond bimbos alongside him, below the company slogan NETWORLD OR BUST, his eyes nearly left their sockets.

"You like those knockers, huh?" Max said.

"Yes, sir, I sure do but—"

"Would you like to meet these girls?"

Long pause, then Kyle asked, "Are they here?"

"No, but I'll tell you what I'll do," Max said. "Next time I'm in Alabama, I'll bring Cindy and Bambi with me, and you can take them up to a room with you, and spend the whole weekend banging their brains out. How'd y'all like that, Kyle?"

"That would be pretty nice," Kyle said. "But when y'all planning to be in Robertsdale again?"

Thinking, When fucking hell freezes, Max said, "Next weekend. I'm here on business and I'll bring the girls with me. What do you say?"

Kyle stared at the monitor for a while longer—did Max see drool? The kid had probably never met a girl outside of church.

Finally Kyle got a hold of himself, said, "Okay, sir. Sounds cool."

Max shook Kyle's hand firmly, sealing the deal. Then Max felt his stomach rumble—the mini-mart on the other side of the office, with the Cheez Whiz and the Pringles and the cans of Bud—especially the cans of Bud—was looking mighty good.

"I'll tell you what, Kyle," Max said. "How about we add a little rider to our deal? Cindy has a twin sister, Lolita, looks exactly like her except her garbanzos are a cup size larger. Lolita loves Southern guys. How about I toss Lolita into the mix and you let me raid the mini-mart this weekend?"

The prospect of three girls at once was too much for Kyle. He looked like he was going to have a stroke, or an orgasm, or *something* massive and, yep, that was drool all right.

He went, "G-g-go on. You can take all the food you want, Mr. Maximilian, sir."

Max went up to his room with a few six-packs of Bud and munchies to last the weekend. He had never been a beer man—the low alcohol content didn't work for him—but as he began to guzzle the brews he found after nine or ten he had a pretty good buzz going. Then he kept up a "maintenance level" of one or two an hour, like he was on alcohol cruise control.

In New York, he'd been eating healthy—well, trying anyway. He had a bad heart; even with Lipitor, his cholesterol was a mess and when was the last time he'd taken Lipitor? The Pop-Tarts alone were probably clogging the shit out of his arteries, but, Eh, the beer was cleaning 'em out. Checks and balances, right? You take some shit, then you wash it down with good vibes. Max was so blasted he had no idea what the fuck any of this meant but, hell, he'd drink to that.

Sometime Friday night, Max passed out. When he woke up on Saturday—unless he'd missed a day, not exactly beyond the realm of possibility—he started drinking again. The routine was getting was old fast, but unless he went sober, he had to keep the brews flowing.

On Sunday night, Max ran out of munchies. He went down to the office, saw the kid at the desk with some black guy. He looked like a gangbanger, with the dreadlocks or whatever, wearing a Denver Nuggets jersey with SPREWELL 8 on the back, and a black stocking on his head. What was up with that anyway? Next thing, they'd be walking around with garters around their necks.

Kyle and the black guy were having a hushed conversation but stopped talking when Max came in. The black guy glared at Max, looking like he wanted to pull out his piece and blow him away. Kyle looked like he was shitting bricks.

"I'll check you later," Kyle said to the black guy, and the guy said, "Yeah, whatever," and walked by Max, bumping into him hard with his shoulder, going, " 'Scuse me," but not like he meant it.

When the black guy was gone, Kyle said to Max, "If you want more Budweiser you can go 'head and take it."

Max, toasted but still plenty with it, went, "What're you doing, making drug deals down here?" He asked it as a joke, but going by the kid's reaction he realized he'd hit the nail on the head. Fuck, Kyle the slow-talking church boy was a dealer. Who would've thought?

"N-n-no, sir," he said, shitting some more bricks. "He's just an, um, old friend'a mine from, uh, high school."

"Don't worry," Max said, "I'm not a fucking narc. C'mon, gimme a break, kid—wise up. If I was a fuckin' cop would I really be hanging out here, OD'ing on

Bud and Cheez Whiz? I mean, going undercover is one thing, but would I torture myself to make a bust? So what kind of shit you dealing? Weed, sense, bud, blow?"

Yeah, that was the way—use all the hip lingo to show the kid he was streetwise, *a player*.

Kyle smiled, said, "Naw, it's not like that, Mr. Maximilian. That there was just my friend, Darnell, and me and Darnell, we was just—"

"Look, you don't gotta bullshit me, all right?" Max said. "Truth is, I've got some dealing experience myself. In seventh grade, I dealt weed, shrooms, and speed. How do you think I got to be such a respected business-man? The drug business is just like any other business. You have a product, you have a customer, and you have margins. I was growing the shit in my closet. Had a tree up to the ceiling, and got some serious bud off it. So you don't have to beat around the bush with me, kid—no pun intended."

Max laughed. Man, he was on fire tonight. Fuckin' smoking. That old Bud, maybe it cleaned out the debris, let his razor-sharp mind get cooking.

Kyle stared at Max for a while, then said, "Can I pat you down?"

"Ah, Jesus Christ," Max said. Then, realizing the kid wasn't joking, went, "Go 'head, go 'head."

Kyle frisked Max, doing it so slow Max started to wonder, Is this kid from Brokeback Mountain or what?

Finally, satisfied Max wasn't a narc, Kyle said, "It was crack, sir."

Max went, "Crack? You're shitting me. Didn't that ro out in the nineties?"

"You'd be surprised," the kid said. "There's still a good market for it. A niche market, but still."

Listen to this kid, *niche market*. Like he was on goddamn CNBC.

"You using or selling?" Max asked.

Kyle hesitated, as if wondering, Maybe it wasn't such a good idea to divulge he was involved in crack deals to a total stranger, even if that total stranger wasn't a narc. Then, looking like he was thinking *Well, told him this much—mise well tell him the rest*, Kyle said, "Selling."

Kyle a crack dealer! Max was beside himself, almost started laughing. He remembered Angela had had a whole other spin on *crack*—freaking mick-speak. Over there, they spelled it *craic*, which meant "party on" or some shit. But why was he thinking about that bitch now?

The kid was asking, "You want to check some out?"

Max had done coke *mucho* times before. Fuck, he'd spent half the eighties at Studio 54 and the Palladium, snorting mountains of blow. But he had enough trouble in his life. He didn't need a goddamn crack habit.

"What do I look like, some low-rent nigger?"

God, had he said that out loud? Hello, filter, where are you? Thank God Darnell wasn't around to hear that one.

"I mean negro," Max said. "I mean person of colored. What-the-fuck-ever."

"Actually," Kyle said, "That attitude is a misperception."

"What is?" Max asked, surprised Kyle knew such a big word. Four syllables—Jesus.

"That African-Americans make up the majority of crack users," Kyle said. "My clientele is all races. Heck, I'm white and I smoke it."

Kyle on crack. This Max had to see.

Max said, "This I have to see."

"You're already seein' it," Kyle said. "I was basin' with Darnell about ten minutes ago."

Max knew Kyle wasn't fucking with him, but he didn't get it. Weren't crackheads supposed to talk fast? This kid sounded like Gomer Fucking Pyle. If this was the way he spoke on crack, Max couldn't imagine how slow his brain worked normally.

Maybe this crack wasn't as powerful as they said it was. Maybe it wasn't all it was cracked up to be.

"Cook me up some of your shit," Max said.

Keeping his tone casual, like he was one cool dude. Like whatever you had, bring it on.

Kyle hung the BE BACK IN FIVE MINUTES sign on the door and took Max to the back room. As Kyle prepared "the rock," he was telling Max all about his dealing business, how he was taking in a grand a weekend and he only worked at the motel so his parents—"I was raised by good ol' God-fearin' Christians" —would think he was holding down a decent job. Max was feeling something he thought he'd forgotten, that elusive goddess—hope. If Kyle could pull down a grand a week as a crack dealer, imagine what a savvy city slicker like Max Fisher could rake in. Was the sky the limit or what?

The pipe was ready. Max took it, then hesitated, wondering if this was such a great idea. After all, he had an addictive personality. Then he thought, C'mon, how was he gonna endorse the product if he couldn't road test it? You gotta try it before you recommend it. That was the first law of the American corporate bible, right?

Max inhaled. A few seconds later he was fucking flying, like he was fucking God. Even better—like he could kick God's ass.

"This shit is good," Max said.

Man, it was great to finally crawl out of the hole, to have that old Max Fisher energy back. Yeah, get all that Bud outa there and put the rock in its place. Talk about wake-up calls. This was the mother of all wake-up calls. Fuck the ashrams and Om sessions—the secret to true enlightenment was a crack pipe. Man, Max's brain was working as fast as it could. Yeah, he could probably go on the wagon for three weeks and he would've still failed a sobriety, but he was thinking one thing—he could make a fortune with this shit.

Max said frantically, "Can Darnell mule this shit up to me in the city? Well, can he or can't he? Answer the goddamn question."

Kyle started to answer, but Max couldn't wait all day for the slow fuck.

Max went, "Say hello to your new business partner," then brought the pipe back up to his lips and took another hit of enlightenment.

Five

He decided to let it slide, let the shades do the talking,
like rock stars did.
KEN BRUEN AND JASON STARR, *Bust*

Slide was getting his shit together. He had his kidnap victim, Angela, tied up in bed, and now he needed some —what did the brothers call it? Oh, yeah, *mo…ti…vation.* Get that Harlem laid-back emphasis going on.

Angela had told him about the guy in the River Inn, calling her a hooker, *dissing her.* Thing was, Slide hadn't offed anyone for, like, eons. What had it been, a week? And he especially hadn't done somebody for, you know, fun. He'd done the last schmucks for cash, but when had he done one for the sheer heat, the rush, that fucking adrenaline gig? That was what he was talking about, brother.

He got his carpet cutter out, honed the edge. The Guards stopped you, you went, "Hey man, I'm a carpet layer, tools of the trade." That he'd never laid anything but broads was beside the point.

He left a note for Angie, after handcuffing her to the bed. Went:

Babe
T.C.B.
El.

In the car, the thought struck him, Would she know that El was the King and that T.C.B. was, like, his mantra?

Sure, for fook's sake. She was a Yank, had to know all that shit.

He got to the River Inn and sure enough, a punk at the counter, sneer in place.

Slide asked, "Got a room, mate?" Using his English accent.

Slide knew if you wanted to make them record books, you better have a shiteload of talents, mimicry for one. The Brit was simple, just act like you had a lump of coal in yer mouth and act like a complete prick. Piece of cake, or rather, piece of crumpet. Jolly fooking hockey sticks.

That Slide was shite at accents never occurred to him.

The counter guy stared at him, as if thinking, *What's with this wanker?* Asked with a smirk, "You got twenty Euro?"

Slide was delighted. The guy was even better than he hoped—he was giving mouth.

Deciding to fuck with him, Slide adopted a timid voice, went, "Why?"

The guy, not hiding his disdain at all now, said, "You got twenty Euro, I might have a room."

Slide took a quick look around. Coast was clear and, best, no CTTV. What'd you expect, the place was a kip.

He plopped a wad of crumpled notes onto the counter, mumbled, "Is that enough for ya?"

The guy sighed—he could have sighed for Ireland—
and leaned down to sort the notes.

Slide grabbed the mother by his lanky hair, going,
"Jeez, you ever hear of shampoo?" and then slit his
throat from left to right. He stepped back, there was
always a geyser. Sure enough, here it came—fucking
fountain of the red stuff, *whoosh*, there she blew. Slide
never ceased to be struck with admiration by the pure
power of the splurt.

The guy was gargling, emitting strangled moans,
and Slide said, "Was gonna let it slide, know what I
mean? Running yer mouth there, mate. Well, let's fix
that. You think?"

He took off the guy's lips. It took a while—harder
than you'd think to slice evenly. Sometimes you got
gum—not chewing gum, the other kind. Though
sometimes you got chewing gum too.

Slide took the fuck's wallet. It had, like, fifteen Euro
and a photo of a dark-haired woman. Slide kept that.
Figured he'd show it to some chick sometime, say the
girl in the photo was his childhood sweetheart who
broke his heart. Always good for a pity fuck, right?

He was outa there, the lips in his jacket. For a
moment, he imagined the lips talking, giving it large.
He had such a hard-on, couldn't wait to ride Angela
with the handcuffs. Then, mid-orgasm, *hers*, he'd kiss
her with the guy's lips, go, "No lip from you now."

She'd get a kick outa that.

Six

It started as kind of a joke, and then it wasn't
funny anymore because money became involved.
Deep down, nothing about money is funny.
CHARLES WILLEFORD, *The Shark-Infested Custard*

Angela tried to open her eyes, couldn't see, and thought, *Jaysus, have I gone blind*? Or, wait, it was the mascara glued solid. She knew she always overdid the goo, an echo back to her brief stint as a goth chick. But no, this was, like, what, her eyes were covered?

And what the hell was up with her right hand, like it was suspended, and when she pulled, she felt metal grate on her wrist. She managed to sit up and, with her left hand, tore off the covering on her eyes. A blindfold? What the fuck? Then it came flooding back.

Slide, the demented bastard, telling her blindfolds were a huge kick and pouring vast amounts of Jameson down her throat, not like she was fighting it. A year of near poverty in Dublin, was she going to turn down some decent hooch? Yeah, right.

But, Jesus, she needed to pee and now.

Then she saw that the handcuff on her right wrist was attached to the bar above the bed. She yanked at it and it chaffed her wrist, probably tore off some skin. She didn't remember agreeing to that kink.

Or had she?

She did remember, after the first time, when he took her fast, doggy-style—that was nice—they did shots of Jameson. Then he suggested another go and, Jaysus, it was even better the second time—hot, heavy, fevered and wild. It had been a while since she'd lost control like that—not since her old boyfriend, Dillon. Dillon had turned out to be a raging psycho but, boy, he knew how to screw.

Slide, it seemed, had a little Dillon in him. She vaguely recall him shouting, "Ride me yah bitch, go on yah wild thing!"

The Irish male—they might not be subtle but, Christ, they sure were vocal. When he came, she felt a delicious frisson, and then he roared, as if he was dying, "Ah sweet mother ah fook me!....Yah hoor's ghost!....Aw bollix, I love yah!....Yah filthy cunt!" Celtic terms of endearment, right?

And the other thing, every one of them, when they had an orgasm, screamed not blue murder but green mothers. Angela shuddered, realizing that the Irish matriarch wasn't exactly what she wanted to think about in the throes of a ferocious hangover.

She roared, "Slide, I want to be released now! Joke's over and goddamn it, I need to pee. You hear me?"

She listened but, nope, no sign of the Irish fucker.

Then she had an epiphany—she no longer thought of her own self as Irish. How did that happen? She'd been raised in New York, in a Greek-Irish home where the Irish influence was the dominant theme. She knew more about the Boyos than the Yankees, and had bodhrans, spoons, accordions, all around the house. Oh, there'd been plenty of melancholy. Everything, we're talking every single thing, was a tragedy. Her dad had always said, Give a mick lots of grief, pain, sorrow and he was as happy as a pig in shite. Maybe all that rain had something to do with it. They had to occupy themselves somehow so they spent their time pissing and moaning. And Jesus, could they moan.

"Slide, you fookin cunt bastard, I'll have your eyes out, ye demented fool!"

Yep, her year in Dublin had literally robbed her of her Irish-ness all right. And she wasn't the only one losing it—the whole fookin country wasn't Irish anymore. Everybody spoke in bad American accents, wore Harvard or Knicks sweatshirts and watched *The OC*, *The Sopranos*, *Deadwood*, and *The Simpsons*. And, get this, on Sundays, Sky TV showed baseball! Irish guys who wouldn't know their Mantle from their Aaron were talking about *stepping up to the base*, *second innings*, *pitchers*, *catchers* and the *World Series*. How fucked is that?

At a pub one night, Angela asked a baseball fan, "What happened to hurling and shillelaghs?" and the guy went, "Shut yer mouth, woman. Jeter's batting."

And, sin of sins, the guy was drinking Coors Light, for God's sake, with a glass of water as a chaser, as if the shite wasn't watered down enough already.

Truth was, Angela missed America. She wanted a real goddamn sandwich. In Ireland, they gave you slices of thin white bread. No rye, no whole wheat, no fookin pumpernickel. Then they added a shaving of something called *ham* and some sort of dead leaf they claimed was lettuce. Lettuce pray for fucking patience! She wanted to go home, get some meatballs and mashed potatoes, where you didn't have to pay for a second shot of coffee, where a hero was a real sandwich and where people spoke real English.

"Slide, you cunt bastard!"

She'd had enough of the game, if that was what this was. She had to pee like hell, and Christ, she needed a hit of nicotine. Yeah, yeah, she'd started smoking again. How could she help it? Despite the ban in Ireland, it seemed the whole country huddled outside pubs, smoking their fool heads off. Then, one night, she'd learned the reason why. Some girl told her it was the new way to hook up—flirting with a smoke. Slirting or some shite they called it. Well, she'd been slirting her ass off and what good did it do her? She was half-drunk, chained naked to a bed in some cabin on the outskirts of Dublin, waiting for a man who was possibly deranged to come free her.

The cigs were on the table, tantalizingly out of reach. If Slide had done that deliberately, she'd cut his balls off. See if she wouldn't.

She roared, "C'mon yah bollix, enough with the screwing around, like hello, game over?" And she figured she must still be a bit drunk as she added in a screech, "What's a gal gotta do to get a drink around here?"

Then she heard a car pulling into the drive. A few

moments later, there he was, and she launched, "Yah prick, yah storming major asshole, yah…"

From the tent in his pants, her tirade was turning him on and, guess what, she was a little heated her own self.

Then he was on her and they were at it like mad things—sweaty, perverted, debauched, and delighted.

Jesus, she was on fire, hollered, "Kiss me yah bollix!" and Slide slipped his hand into his pocket and then seemed to rub something onto his lips. She thought, *Chapstick now?*

Then he was kissing her. Felt weird, kinda cold— was it some new kind of oral condom or something? And, fuck, she still had to mention the little item of her having, um, you know, herpes.

Before she could say anything, he whispered, "Lips to die for," and he was between her legs again, giving it, as the Brits say, *large*.

God, she roared like a hyena. And, Jesus, those lips—it was like Angelina Jolie was going down on her.

When he'd finally surfaced, he tossed something into the litter bin, said, "Loose lips sink ships."

The fuck was he on about? He got out of bed and she admired his bod. Then he was uncuffing her and she finally got to have that pee. When she returned, he had two cigs lighted and there was a glint in his eye. If she didn't know better, she'd have suspected he wanted to burn her. Yeah, like she was going to let that happen. In New York, she'd dated a married Puerto Rican guy for a while. Not one of her better choices in men but, hey, he looked kind of like Ricky Martin. Okay, in the right light, from the right angle, with beer goggles, but she'd been in a slump with the guys. One night he whispered to her in a sexy Latino tone, "You wanna golden shower, baby." Not as a question, but as if saying, You're getting a golden shower and now. Christ, she was so innocent then. She thought they'd cover themselves in gold leaf or something, hop in the shower and, like, well, maybe lick it off each other. You know, something romantic. So imagine her shock when he'd started pissing on her. She went along with it—what the hell?—but when he broke the news about his family in San Juan she kicked him right in the nuts, shouted, "You won't be pissing, golden or otherwise, for a Spanish month, yeh bastard!"

If Slide tried to burn her, God help him.

But, no, he let her take one of the cigs. As she took a long drag of it, he said, "Let's go out, have a jar, I want to run something by you."

She thought, *The romantic fool, is it marriage*? She knew she'd been good in bed, but was she *that* good? She'd only known him what, a few hours, but, hell, she wasn't about to let an opportunity like this slip away. She didn't want to be one of those single women in their forties who look back at their lives, regretting the one that got away. Though she had some, well, concerns about Slide, she had a gut feeling that he was a good man, and would make a wonderful father. Her gut feelings had rarely been right, but she figured, bad luck didn't last forever, right?

The place was called the Touchdown Bar and Grill.

As they got out of the car, Angela went, "Jeez, how Irish is that?"

A huge sign inside proclaimed, KARAOKE TONIGHT, and she wondered, Were they, like, trying to scare business away?

The place was hopping—three deep at the bar and all shouting for Bud Light, Corona, and Miller.

On the stage, a middle aged woman, looking like a very poor man's Desperate Housewife, was massacring "I Will Survive."

Angela shouted at the stage, "Not if you don't stop that singing, you won't!"

When the woman got to the part about how she was going to walk out the door, Angela said, "You and me both, lady," and then she said to Slide, "I need some air. There's a pub down the road, how about we go there instead?"

Slide wasn't keen but she rubbed his crotch, purred, "If staying here is what you want, then, okay."

She was wondering, Does he have a ring? If he did, it better be a fookin' diamond—a big one. And if he was the typical Irishman and tried to propose to her with a Claddagh ring, Lord help him.

Slide led her through the crowd, going, "Lady coming through."

They found a space at the bar, ordered large Bush-mills with Guinness chasers.

She whined, "Don't I get to choose my own drink?"

He shoved her glasses at her, said, "You have what I have."

Mr. Taking Command, but she liked it.

A huge painting of—what else?—a baseball player hung on the wall and Slide sneered, "I see your point about this baseball shite, babe. What do we know about American sport?"

Without thinking, Angela corrected, "*Sports*. We say American *sports*."

Slide gave her a look that shouted, *Never correct my American again, ever*.

Then he toasted, "Here's looking at you, kiddo."

She was going to correct him, go, It's *kid*, but had a feeling she'd better keep her mouth shut.

They did a few more of The Bush and that sucker slid on down so easy, packed its own potent wallop. Next thing, Slide was on stage, doing "My Way," the anthem of macho losers the world over. He wasn't awful but, then again, anything was a relief after having to listen to that dame sing disco.

Angela felt eyes on hers and saw a well-dressed guy smiling at her. She noticed the gold Rolex and the deep tan. Yeah, he was a player. And he had great teeth. In Ireland, that translated as, Cash and lots of it.

In the back of her mind, she was already thinking, *Slide? Slide who?*

Then Slide was back, asking, "Did you like my singing?"

She gushed, "God, it was beautiful, you could make a career of it."

Dumb fuck believed her too. Was there one man on the goddamn planet who if you told him he was the greatest, didn't buy it?

He gave a *Gee shucks* almost shy grin, said, "Remind

me to do 'Stairway to Heaven' for you, I improvise all
the instruments too."

She suppressed a shudder, went, "I can hardly wait."

Slide got a six-pack to go and they were in the
parking lot, his hands all over her.

Then they heard, "Hey, wait up," and saw the Rolex
guy swaggering over.

"Hey, where you dudes headed?"

Dudes, with a thick Irish accent.

Slide thumbed a bottle from the six, asked, "Like a
brew, dude?" Then he smashed the bottle on the car,
put the jagged shards into the guy's face.

Grinding the bottle in, he went, "There you go,
dude, it's Miller time."

Then he took the guy's wallet and Rolex and shouted
to Angela, "Get in the car, we're so outa here. You
drive, baby."

Looking at the wailing guy trying to pull the bottle
out of his face, she said, "But, Slide, why did you have
to—"

"I said get in the fookin' car and drive, woman."

Angela got in. It took her a moment to figure out
the gears, as she was accustomed to automatic. But by
luck more than skill she got the thing in gear and got
out of there, fast.

Slide was going through the guy's wallet, shouting,
"Jesus wept, there is a god, there's a shitpile of cash in
here, this bastard was seriously carrying, you know
what this means, babe?"

She knew what it meant—her new boyfriend was
seriously deranged. The casual violence, the way he'd

chopped down the poor guy. There was something romantic about it, but still.

She said, "Did you have to, you know, go so far?"

Slide gave her a mega smile, crooned, "I did it my way."

Slide was modeling the Rolex, turning it on his wrist, letting the light bounce off of it. Angela was thinking, *So, how come you get the watch? You wanna tell me that?*

But Slide was high all right—wired on the blood and the violence, pacing the room, his eyes neon lit with frenzy. Once again, he was seriously reminding Angela of Dillon, that psycho poet nut job, but it was possible that Slide was even more out there, really way perched on the precipice.

Now he was speaking, the words spilling over themselves, tumbling out like floods of rap dementia, going, "Babe, we're a team, we're on a hot streak and we should keep the level up and I have just the plan to get us some serious wedge, how do you feel about kidnapping?"

And she thought, Kidnapping, another term for marriage without the rings.

She said, "Wait, you mean how do I feel about you kidnapping me?"

"No," he snapped as if she'd asked a stupid question. "How do you feel about joining up with me in the kidnapping biz?"

So, what, now she was going to be the Irish version of Patty Hearst? Least she'd remember to wash her hair.

What was that girl thinking, letting CCTV pick her up on a bad hair day. Christ, you rob a bank, at least make the effort, put a little blusher on, a hint of eyeliner.

She went, "Kidnapping biz?"

He slowed a tad, said, "You'll have noticed the chains and shite around the house, right?"

Like you could miss them?

Before she could say, You mean it wasn't a kink? he went, "I'm in the kidnapping biz, a pro, been doing it for a while."

And fuck, he looked so proud, like he was really doing something important, his bit for the new prosperity. Meanwhile, she was thinking, *And how successful have you been? You live in a shithole, can barely buy the drinks, drive a freaking banger, and have to roll some poor schmuck in a car park.*

Here he was again, now looking like he was about to bestow some great honor, going, "I've decided to let you be my partner."

She loved *decided*. Like he'd been deliberating over it and wasn't she lucky she'd been *picked*.

Then she thought, A kidnapper, an Irish well-groomed version of Patty Hearst. She had to admit, there was something glamorous about it. And if you did it right, shite, there could be a real payoff. Christ, wouldn't she just kill to be rich?

She asked, "But nobody gets hurt, right?"

He gave her a bashful smile, said, "See, that's my motto right there, no pain, lotsa gain."

This from a guy who put broken bottles in strangers' faces.

She went, "You're a caring man."

He literally hung his head, whispered, "I put the C in care. Sometimes, I think I care too much."

She nodded, thinking the C applied if you meant cunt, then asked, "Have you someone in mind?"

He sang, "*You can always get what you want.*"

Real pleased he was using *can*, not *can't*.

Then, scaring the shite out of her, he did a hip swivel that was supposedly Jagger, but came off like Jim Carrey in *The Mask*.

"Go on," she said. "Who?"

"Who?" he said. "Jagger or Richards, one of those fookers. The Stones are in town, and someone'd pay plenty to get those lads back alive."

"The Rolling Stones," she said.

He looked at her, nodded.

She said, "You want to kidnap the Rolling Stones? That's your plan?"

"The fook's wrong with it?" he said.

The idea started to grow on her. The Stones weren't so young anymore, probably couldn't run like they'd've been able to back when.

But would there be room here for the lads? And of course she'd need a whole new wardrobe. Mick liked his women in the newest gear. God, she was already seeing Mick's lips on her neck. So, okay, he had a few wrinkles but fuck, he still had those buns and, come on, if you haven't sucked a Stone, have you really lived? Have you?

She could see herself on *Oprah*, Oprah's fattish face, full of curiosity, asking, *And when did Mick give you the diamond ring?* Then Angela would modestly flash the huge stone on her engagement finger. She'd make a joke about it, go, "I've got my Stone all right." She pictured her and Mick spending winters in the south of France, and lots of little Stones with Angela's eyes.

"So what do you say?" Slide said. "You in or out?"

Imagining herself and Mick getting married on an exclusive island off the coast of Who The Fook Cares, Angela sang in a voice much worse than Slide's: *"Wild horses…won't keep me away…"*

Seven

"OK," I said. "Forget the whole thing."
"Really?"
"Order are orders," I said. "The alternative is
anarchy and chaos."
LEE CHILD, *The Enemy*

Max Fisher was the shit all right. He was living it up—
the kingpin of New York, another goddamn Scarface.
His crib—he called it FisherLand—was a penthouse
sublet on East Sixty-sixth Street and Second Avenue.
He'd always liked the building because it was made of
dark black glass, like the windows of a limo, and to
Max, it oozed class, was a place The Donald would've
loved before he started naming buildings after himself.

Yeah, everything was going Max's way, all right. He
was making five grand a week in profit as what he liked
to call himself, "a high-end crack dealer." He had the
freshest clothes, a live-in sushi chef named Katsu, and
best of all he was getting some of the finest poontang
in the city from his steady ho, Felicia, a former stripper
he'd known from Legz Diamond.

Yeah, it was hard to believe how far Max's life had
come since that weekend from hell in Alabama.

How many other slick brothers like himself could've
got out of that hole? No cash, a chink in your ass, literally, and not only had he kissed that shithole goodbye,

but he'd set up a mini-empire in Manhattan. And we're not talking years here, buddy. He'd put this shit together in—what was it that Irish cunt used to say?—oh, yeah, *jig time*.

Where was that Irish bitch now? he wondered. If the curse he'd paid to have put on her worked, she was probably in an Irish prison, sucking some prison guard's meat in the hope of a free lunch. Yeah, Angela had fucked Max over but good, but who was laughing now, bitch? Who was the player in the toughest game in town and who was on her knees, taking it large in some skank Irish prison? Huh? Huh?

Man, if Max had known the crack business would be such a gold mine, he wouldn't have wasted years of his life selling goddamn computer networks.

The thing was, unlike a lot of businesses, it was so easy to get the ball rolling as a crack dealer. The start-up costs were miniscule, and the obstacles to entry were virtually non-existent. All he needed was product and steady customers. And the great thing about the business was you didn't have to worry about shit like "competing technology." Once you hooked a customer, he was yours for life.

The way Max got the action started: a week after he'd hightailed it out of Alabama, Kyle had sent a mule, some high school kid, up to the city with Max's first supply of rock. He had the merchandise; all he needed was the customers. In his days as head honcho, Max had had to do with whatever was necessary to close sales, including, for many important clients, scoring coke. Max figured that all had to do was "transition" the fucks from coke to crack and he'd make a mint. Easy, right? And of course Kyle had been all for the idea, even though the putz was only getting twenty percent, and it was twenty percent of the *profits*, and Max had no intention of paying it to him anyway. Poor fuckin' Kyle. The kid was so in love with the idea of having a foursome with the blond bimbos that if Max had told him to go up to Harlem and stand in front of the Magic Johnson movie theater wearing a FUCK YOU, NIGGERS T-shirt, the stupid moron would've done it.

But, yeah, Max's drug dealing business was a huge hit. He started small, with addicts he knew. Like one of his oldest steadies, Jack Haywood. Jack was the VP of Information Technology at a major midtown invest-ment banking firm. He was a closet cokehead and Max had been taking advantage of this for years, plying the asshole with coke and table dances in exchange for inking six- and seven-figure IT deals.

So when Max had received his first shipment of rock, he'd called Jack at work and gone, "Don't hang up on me. I've got something good for you—"

"I can't do business with you any more," Jack said nervously.

"It's not about business," Max said. "It's—"

"I'm sorry," Jack said. "It's not you. I think you're a decent guy, but my bosses—they don't want me, well, associating with you anymore."

Max had expected this attitude from Jack. When NetWorld had gone under, Max had gotten into a little trouble with the police. Something about a bunch of murders he didn't commit. None if it had been any fault of his—blame it on booze and that ditzy bitch, Angela. Call it "the dark period" in his life. But that was all in the past. He was a new Max Fisher now, a Max Fisher who had discovered the wonderful world of crack cocaine.

"It's not what you think," Max said. "I just want to get together, for old time's sake."

"I'm sorry, I can't—"

"I have some new candy for you," Max said.

Candy was the old code word that Max and Jack used to have for coke.

There was silence on the line, then Jack said, "I don't like candy any more," but Max could tell the idea was very appealing to him.

"This is really sweet, really delicious candy," Max said. "I tried some myself the other day."

A longer silence, then Jack asked, "How sweet and how delicious?"

Max punched the air, thinking, *Gotcha, sucker.* What was that line from *House of Games,* and two to take 'em? No, that wasn't it. What-the-fuck-ever.

Max took Jack out, got him hooked. Before long, Jack was spending a thou a week on Max's shit, and that was only one customer. Soon Max had twelve other Jack Haywoods and his profits started to explode. Hell, Jack had even hooked his wife on crack. That was the beauty of the business—you could gain new customers so effortlessly. It was all word of mouth. You didn't need to advertise, you didn't need to invest a lot of money in having a pretty office. There was no one

to impress. All you had to do was get people addicted
and you were golden. They would get others hooked,
and so on and so on. This was better than TiVo and the
George Foreman Grill.

Max had been smoking crack himself—but he was
taking it easy, kept it to two pipes a day. Well, maybe
more than that sometimes, but he didn't go crazy or
anything. He found that crack actually kept him bal-
anced. If he was having too much booze, he would
smoke a crack pipe to pull himself back up, and vice
versa. It kept him levelheaded, in control. And, just
like he was avoiding mixing alcohol, he stuck to crack
and crack only. The stupid fuckers who got addicted to
the rock—like Jack Haywood and his wife—were the
ones who cut it with brown. Yeah, that was right, Max
called heroin *brown*. He was up on all the current, hip
drug lingo all right. He listened to Naz, Ja Rule, Busta
Rhymes, and 50 Cent. He even knew how many times
50 had been shot—nine. See how hip he was?

To keep the hip vibes flowing, he had gangsta
movies playing on his massive Sony 64-inch LCD TV,
twenty-four-seven. Classics like *Boyz n the Hood*,
Menace II Society, *Gang Related*, and, of course, the
granddaddy of 'em all, *Scarface*. One of Max's favorite
ways to pass the time was to smoke some good rock
while watching *Scarface* and trying to keep track of
how many *putas* Pacino blows away. When he got into
the twenties he always lost count.

Max learned lots of hip lingo, but *chill*—ah, chill
was by far his favorite new word. Man, he loved saying
chill. And it was such a useful word; it had so many

meanings. Chill could mean to relax, as in, "Chill out, my man" or "I'm just sitting in here in FisherLand, chillin' with my bee-atch." But it also meant to be cool, like, "I'm chill, baby, I'm chill." And it meant, "Hang out," like when you say to somebody, "Wanna chill?" But the best way to use chill was in place of fuck. Like sometimes Max would go to Felicia, "Yo wassup, my bee-atch? You wanna get in bed and chill, baby?" Or sometimes, while she was going down on him, Max, high on crack, would go, "Yeah, chill on my rod for a while, baby. Yeah, like that, my bee-atch."

Was hiring Felicia as his round-the-clock ho the best move he'd ever made or what?

When the money started rolling in, one of the first things Max had done was go to Legz Diamond in midtown, where he used to entertain his networking clients back in the day. He bought a lap dance from Felicia, and as she was squatting over him, those great fake tits—had to be quadruple Ds—inches away from his face, he whispered to her, "Can I ask you a personal question?"

"They ain't real," she said.

"I know that," Max said. "I was curious about something else. How much're you making?"

She thought about it, went, "You mean dancin'?"

"No, I mean the whole enchilada. Dancing plus whatever else you do on weekends. How much you make in a week?"

After a long pause, she went, "On a good week? Two thousand."

Max went, "Say hello to your new boss—I'm paying you four."

And that was it, done deal. Talk about closing a sale.

Felicia moved into the penthouse with him and Max only had one rule: she had to walk around topless at all times. He didn't care what she wore on the bottom, but he needed to see those tits constantly. Her knockers were like his goddamn *inspiration*. He could be feeling down about something, self-doubt creeping in, and he'd go, "Yo, Felicia, come here bee-atch and chill on my lap," and life would have meaning again.

The most chill thing about Felicia was how she knew her place in the world, and how she accepted it. She knew she was a ho, a bee-atch, and she didn't give Max "no talkin' back to." Most of the other women in his life had been a lot more sensitive. Angela, forget about it. If he called her a bee-atch, she'd would've bashed his face in. And his ex-wife Deirdre, God rest her soul, hadn't exactly rolled with the punches either. If Max had let one slip, called her a cunt or something, she would've had a big fit, going on about how he was "verbally abusive" and "a misogynist" and a "womanizer." Yadda, yadda, yadda. Thank God he was through with all of that shit, right?

But, yeah, Max was in heaven with Felicia. If there was such a thing as an ideal woman she was it. At home, it was like she was his beck-and-call girl, his Pretty Black Woman, but nothing had ever made him feel more like a player than the times he took her out on the town. He'd be in one of his new mustard-colored suits, and she'd be wearing something really skimpy, showing as much of her boobs as was legally allowed, and just to see the looks on people's faces was priceless. Everybody was so fucking jealous, especially the guys. They'd look at him, their mouths sagging open, and he could read their minds. All the jealous fucks were wishing that they could be Max Fisher, just for one day, just to see what it was like.

Sometimes Max took Felicia out clubbing to all the hip spots. Max felt like he was back in the good ol' days at Studio 54. So what if he was the oldest guy on the dance floor and the kids called him "Gran'pa"? Max Fisher still knew how to get jiggy wid it and he and Felicia had a fucking blast.

But Max's favorite place to take her to, to be seen, was the QT hotel on Forty-fifth Street. There was a hip swimming pool bar on ground level in the lobby and it was where all the current happening players hung out with their beautiful young ho's.

Businessmen on their lunch breaks would stop by, not to swim, but just to leer in through the glass at the spectacular women in bikinis, wishing that some day their wildest dreams would come true and that they could score some of that fine poontang for themselves.

Max knew what it was like because he used to be one of those losers himself. But now he'd turned the tables. Now he was the one in the water with his beautiful smoking hot bee-atch, and the guys in suits were looking in at him. Man, it felt good to be a winner, on the other side of the glass.

The only little issue Max had had with Felicia was one day when he went into his safe in his office to put away some cashish, and noticed the wedge of green

was looking a little low. He did a count and sure
enough a thousand bucks was missing.

He said, "That fuckin' *puta*'s stealing from me?"

Sounding like Pacino without even trying.

He went under his bed, took out his rod. You wanna
be a drug lord, you better talk the talk. Max knew shit
about guns, had never even fired one, but man, just
holding a piece in his hand made him feel like his dick
was six inches longer. Which would make it, what, a
solid nine-and-a-half inches?

He started toward the bathroom where Felicia was
showering, then he decided he needed to get pumped
for this. He hadn't smoked any crack in about an
hour—Jesus, it was like he was going cold turkey. He
didn't have time to cook up some shit, so he took out
the little silver wrapper, did some fast lines. This was
nothing like the rock, barely a notch above a double
espresso, but, man, it hit him like a train, fast and
hard. He did a little dance, rapping a little of the
gangsta stuff he'd been listening to, doing a little 50
Cent. He sounded great and thought he could release
a rap album and it would go fuckin' platinum. But he'd
need a cool name, have to use numbers or initials or
something. What about M.A.X.? Yeah, that had a ring
to it and man, he could rap. He'd go on stage in a
suit—didn't P. Daddy, or whatever the hell his name
was today, do that?

But Max knew if he wanted to go gangsta he'd have
to take it all the way. He'd get all the right threads. Shit,
when he was The Man, the designers would be giving

him clothes for free—they'd want their clothes to *be seen* on The M.A.X. He liked that, put *The* in front of his name, to highlight that he was the one and only M.A.X., the *official* M.A.X., that there was no other. Yeah, and he'd have buy a Jeep, get some customized *The M.A.X.* plates for it. Man, would that look bitchin' or what? He laughed, *bitchin'*. He was getting' down with the homies all right. The coke loosening him, he was flying, ideas hitting him, like a zillion a second. When he was a big-time rap star he knew all the brothers, all the bee-atches, would look up to him, like he was a mother who'd been around the block a few times and they best be showin him some respect. Yeah, he'd seen that respect, no, *fear*, from his bee-atch, Felicia. Her eyes fucking dazzled at his genius. They'd be in the hood, hanging with his homies, and he'd be her Mr. Wall Street. Like how many guys could pull off corporate America and be down with the gangstas? Yeah, it was time to pull some attitude on that sista.

Max went into the bathroom, slid open the shower door, and pointed the gun right at her face, holding it sideways, the way the brothers did.

He went, "You wanna get up in my face, bee-atch? Or maybe you wanna suck on some of dis?"

Not this—*dis*.

Felicia knew she was in some deep shit. She started begging, *pleading* for him to put the gun down, going "Don't do nothin' crazy" and "Don't shoot me, please don't shoot me." It was great watching her squirm, being at his mercy. Now he knew what Pacino was talking about. Guns, drugs, tits and rap—what else did a man need?

Max went, "Where's my fuckin' money, bee-atch!"

He was so juiced he nearly squeezed off a round. Saw himself as Pacino, going, *Fuck you, how's at?* And blowing the *puta* away.

She was still begging: "I swear to you, baby. I didn't take nothing. Why I need yo' money? You be givin' me so much already. Think about it. You know that shit's stupid, right?"

She went on, whining, and Max felt like he was losing his edge. Why did he do that bullshit coke? He couldn't wait to get his lips around that fucking crack pipe.

He interrupted whatever she was babbling about and screamed at her, "I got ears, ya' know! I hear things!"

Shit, Pacino again.

"I don't know what the hell you talkin' 'bout," she said. "Just get that gun out my damn face! Get it out my face!"

"What happened to my fuckin' money?"

"How I know what happen to it? I ain't seen it. How'd I even get in yo' damn safe? I don't know the combination. I don't know what you even accusin' me for, pointin' a gun in my fuckin' face like a crack-up, dumb ass, street ho motherfucker."

Desperate for some rock, feeling dizzy, Max went, "I know I'm a thousand bucks short."

Felicia fired back, "So why you think I took it? Maybe yo' damn sushi chef stole it."

Max thought about this. Katsu steal from him? It didn't add up but, hell, nothing added up right now.

"What the fuck ever," Max said. "But if I ever find any money missing you better watch your ho ass because next time you won't be so lucky. Next time I'm gonna slap you silly."

Later on, when he finally got some good crack into his system, Max wished he could've taken that last line back. *Slap you silly*. That didn't sound hip and cool at all. What the hell had he been thinking? He worried if this was a side effect of crack. It was supposed to speed you up, but it seemed to be slowing him down. Maybe that explained Kyle.

It had to be the crack because Max used to be the type of guy who could always think of the "big line" at the right time. Like when he was working in sales, going for the bulldog close, his brain never failed him. But now, lately—well, in the last couple minutes anyway—he was losing his edge.

He had to get the crack out of his system, get some food into the mix.

"Katsu, get your nip ass out here!"

Max's sushi chef came into the living room, bowed. Max liked that—showing his boss respect.

"Make me three spider rolls," Max said. "Pronto. And skimp on the caviar again, I'll shoot you. Got that, slant eyes?"

Jeez, did he really say slant eyes? He took a deep breath, thinking, *Easy, big guy. Chill*.

"Yes, Mr. Fisher," Katsu said. "I make spider roll for you right now, Mr. Fisher."

"It's The M.A.X.," Max said. "My name's initials now with 'The' in front of it. Got that?"

Katsu bowed and went into the kitchen to make the sushi.

The missing thousand bucks was still eating away at Max. A business was like a ship. When there was a hole you had to plug it up fast or the whole fucking thing would go down.

Max went into the kitchen, said to Katsu, "You didn't happen to pocket a thousand G's of my moolah, did you?"

Katsu looked confused. What now? He's accused of stealing, suddenly the skinny little nip can't speak English?

Max took out his piece, jammed the muzzle into Katsu's ear and said, "You best not be lying or I'll slap you silly. I mean, I'll slap you really hard. I mean, I'll... Ah, fuck..."

Marching out of the kitchen, he couldn't believe he'd blown the big line again. He had to cut down on the crack. There was no doubt about it, it was fucking up his brain big time.

He needed an antidote—a little weed, or throw some Valium into the mix. You can never be too mellow. Mellow yellow Max—that would be his new thing. Fuck, rap, it was horseshit anyway. He'd go acoustic, sing peace songs. C'mon, how hard was it to sound better than Cat Stevens anyway?

Yeah, the Val was kicking in and Max was chilling big time now. Easing on down the road, he cracked open a bottle of Merlot. Wine had become his drink of choice. Had to lay off the hard stuff and after Alabama he didn't want to see another bottle of Bud for as long as he lived. But you want the class and culture of wine you gotta fucking show it. So he had bought a shitpile of Merlot, had racks of it on display. He knew Merlot was where it was at after he saw that movie, *Sideways*. What was wrong with that idiot anyway? The divorced blond chick was horny as hell, wanted to fuck him stupid, and he kept blowing her off? And Max was supposed to take wine advice from that loser?

Max poured a large glass, took a lethal wallop. He swirled a little of the stuff in his mouth and didn't they spit it out then and say, tad fruity?

He spit some out and said, "Tad fruity?"

Then he made *mmmph* sounds and swirled some more, went "1987, late fall," then said, "Ah, fuck it," and drained the glass in one gulp.

He felt the munchies coming on fast and, thank God, Katsu brought out the spider rolls just in time.

"Sorry about before," Max said, going for a super smooth, jazz musician-type voice, like he was a DJ on fucking Lite FM. "Katsu, I think you're a really cool cat, man. I didn't mean to frighten you or anything with that gun. That was just the crack talking, that wasn't me. But I'm chill now, I'm real chill. So what do you think, man? We chill?"

"Yes, we are chill," Katsu said, and he bowed and returned to the kitchen.

Max wolfed down the sushi—man, that was good

shit, but he was starting to get sick of it. He'd been having sushi three meals a day for, what, two months? It was classy food, but still.

Scarface was playing on the TV. For a little change of pace, Max put in *Carlito's Way*. What could he say, he couldn't get enough of Pacino. And come to think of it, didn't he and Al look more than a little alike? Yeah, they both had that smoldering gig going on, the half-lidded eyes.

Max whispered, *"You wanna piece of me?"*

Maybe Pacino would play Max in the movie of his life. And, make no mistake, Max's life was ripe for the big screen. They loved riches-to-rags-to-riches stories, didn't they? And, whoa, hold the phones, what about HBO? His life could be a series—God knew there were enough plot twists—and he had a title already, *Maxwood*. Speaking of which, he was starting to pop a little wood.

"Beeeee-atch!"

Max called for Felicia again and a couple of minutes later she was busy on her knees, chilling. It was great to have things back to normal with his bee-atch and he could tell she was digging the whole mellowed-out Max Fisher deal. Had to be better than having a gun in her face anyway.

Later on, he and Felicia were chilling with Merlot, watching Pacino, when the phone rang.

"Maximilian?"

It was fucking Kyle.

Shit, had the pot and the Val brought him that far down? It even seemed like Kyle was talking fast.

"My name's not Max, it's The M.A.X."

"Oh, sorry 'bout that, sir, I guess I have the wrong number."

"It's me, you stupid fucking moron," Max said, thinking was this a put-on or what? Could a human being be this retarded? "Hey, and I was about to call you. Where is the mule with my candy? We were supposed to do that deal today? Ten grand, remember?"

"That's why I'm calling," Kyle said. "I have some bad news for you about that."

Felicia was eating a spider roll, not paying attention.

"I'm warning you," Max said. "I'm an emotional guy lately. You don't want to say anything that might rub me the wrong way."

"I can't send you any more candy, sir."

"Maybe it's the Southern accent or the insane amount of coke I've done today, but I don't think I understood you. I thought you just said you·can't send me any more candy."

"I'm sorry," Kyle said. "It's out of my hands."

"Whoa, whoa, what the fuck're you talking about, 'any more'? You trying to say you're cutting me off? No one cuts off The M.A.X.!"

Looked like mellow Max Fisher was a thing of the past. That didn't last long.

"Please don't be mad at me, sir," Kyle said. "It's not my fault, sir."

"Who is it then? Is it that nigger, Darnell?"

Felicia gave Max a nasty look. Max mouthed, *Sorry*. Should've added, My bee-atch.

"No it's not Darnell either, sir. It's our friends in

Colombia. They don't…maybe we shouldn't be talking about this on the phone."

"Paranoia's no way to live your life, Kyle. What the fuck is the Colombians' problem?"

"Well, they don't trust you, sir. They said until they get a chance to meet you we can't send it up to you in New York."

"Did you tell them who they're dealing with?"

Long pause, then Kyle said, "I told them your name."

"Not my name, you idiot. Did you tell them who I *am*. Did you tell them I'm a mogul, I'm a kingpin, that I'm a respected businessman, that nobody ever, ever calls the shots with The M.A.X.?"

"I'm sorry, sir," Kyle said. "I'm just reportin' the facts as the facts were reported to me."

"Stop the slow talk and just fucking listen to me," Max said. "I have twenty grand sitting here and I have no candy. Do you understand my predicament? I have customers who have very sweet tooths, or teeth, or whatever the fuck, and I need to get them their god-damn candy."

"Maybe if we can arrange a meeting—"

"You mean an audition? I don't audition for nobody."

Did Pacino ever say that? If not, he should've.

"I'm sorry, Max…I mean, The M.A.X. If they can't meet you, they won't do the deal."

Max let out an angry breath, shook his head, said, "If those cocksuckers think I'm going down to Alabama they're out of their minds."

Yeah, that was the way—put the peons in their place. *Peons*—he liked that, but he wasn't sure what it meant. Did it mean people you pee on? Yeah, probably.

Kyle was saying, "They said they want me to bring them up to New York. Somethin' about how they want to see you on your own turf or somethin', see what you're all about."

"I hope you realize how insulting this is," Max said. "But if you think I'm letting them walk into my apartment you're out of your mind. I'm not letting any scummy Colombians into FisherLand. Dis be my crib, homey. You all wan' in, you waits like for the in-vite."

Felicia was still on the couch next to Max. He didn't want her listening in on his important business and said to Kyle, "Wait a second," then went to Felicia, "Baby, do me a favor, and chill in the bedroom, okay?"

She got up slowly and Max watched her walk away. There was no question she had all-star knockers, but her ass was on the big side; you might even call it fat. He'd have to have a little talk with her about that at some point. Maybe she'd have to cut down on the desserts, start using Splenda.

When Felicia was gone Max said to Kyle, "Okay, here's the way we're gonna work it. They can come to my town. That's right, New York is my town, I fuckin' own it. But we do it on my terms. I pick the time and the spot and I'll let them know what the time and the spot is when I want to tell them what the time and the spot is. You got that?"

Yeah, this was the old wheeler and dealer talking. Nobody could pull a power play on The M.A.X.

"I'll let them know all that," Kyle said. "But there's just one other thing."

"Yeah, what is it? Come on, talk, I don't have all day."

"You think, maybe, when I come up to New York you might have the girls there ready for me?"

Max didn't know what Kyle was talking about, said, "What the hell're you talking about?"

"You know," Kyle said, "the girls from the Internet— the ones on the Porsche and the sister too. Bambi? Cause you said you were gonna bring 'em down here, but you never did and—"

"Have you ever heard the word chill, Kyle?"

"Yes, sir, but—"

"I have the girls all primed up, ready to meet you. Bambi was just saying to me the other day, 'Why can't I meet Kyle already? I really want to meet him.' And I went to her, 'Easy, baby. Chill.' And now I'm telling you the same thing."

Long dead silence then Kyle went, "I don't get it. So the girls'll be waitin' for me up in New York City?"

"Only if you stay chill," Max said, and clicked off.

Max got up. Whoa, nelly. He felt a little unsteady but, hey, you're doing major, like, biz with Colombians, you're gonna be a tad unsteady. Shit, there was that *tad* again, his inner Brit coming out.

Then it suddenly hit him and he screeched, "Fucking Colombians!"

Was he in the big time now or what? Colombians, fucking drug lords, were coming up to the city to meet with him. This was his moment, his time. Like Pacino, he'd eat the savages for fucking breakfast. Didn't

Pacino take all these dudes *mano a mano*? Wait, that was Cubans, not Colombians. Eh, same shit.

Yeah, everything was going The M.A.X.'s way now. Keep Kyle happy, get him some sleazy hookers, let them fuck him stupid. Well, could he be more stupid? Now he was sounding like Chandler from *Friends*. How talented could one man be? Voices, business acumen, well hung, and he was a good man too, promoting diversity in his work force. Christ, he wanted to hug himself.

He shouted, "Yo, bee-atch! Git yo' sweet ass in here, de man need his pipes blown!"

Maybe he'd let the ho sit on his face, she liked that, and she sure had enough on there to cover his neck as well.

He took off his boxers and settled back on the couch. Shut off Pacino, put on Snoop Dog for some *mood*.

His stomach rumbled, all that goddamn sushi. Fuck the diet food, an *hombre* like him needed some goddamn calories. He could see a porterhouse steak, mashed potatoes, mountain of gravy and some heavy wedge of cheesecake to top it off. Needed some meat on his bones to deal with the *Cubanos*.

Felicia came into the living room. Looked great topless but, man, that ass.

She went, "You ready for me, baby?"

Time for a little *Scarface*. Max, in his best Tony Montana, went, "Okay, fuck me, how's 'at?"

Eight

Slide was waiting at the bottom of Grafton Street. He looked around, making sure no one was in sight, then ducked into the alley that runs alongside the rear entrance to Lily's Bordello. *Lily's!* The hottest venue in Dublin, where Bono held court and any celebrity just had to show up. You did a gig in Dublin, it was *de rigeur* to hit Lily's after. Slide had heard that the Stones were in town and he knew those geriatric bastards would have to show up at Lily's after their gig.

Slide muttered, "You better fooking believe it."

His plan, half baked as usual, was to nab Keif—Keith Richards. Figured Mick had too big a posse but Keith—yeah, he was getable. This alleyway, with the new smoking ban in force everywhere, was where the celebs nipped down for a hit of the nicotine or weed or what-the-fook-ever they were inhaling. Keith, he'd be first down, grab his own self some major drag of some substance, and Slide would be waiting. He'd grab him fast, get the fook outa Dodge.

Jaysus, how much would the Stones pay to get the Keifer back? Slide's mind boggled at the prospect of, like, millions! Then fecking Mick Jagger would bankroll his record-breaking killing spree. Satisfaction that.

The side door opened and in the half-light he saw a thin figure, leather jacket, shades, white hair, skinny as a rodent, lined face. Shit, it looked like someone took a cookie cutter and drew deep wedges on his cheeks.

Slide was momentarily taken from left field, thinking, *Has to be Keifer*.

They say the camera adds twenty pounds, so it figured in person he'd look damn near anorexic. Or *damn near dead* was more like it. Sure enough, Slide heard a click of a Zippo, that was the clincher. Keith would definitely be a Zippo kind of dude.

Slide pulled the black sack from his jacket, moved like a shark, had the bag over the guy's head and shoulders and chest in jig time. But was he breathing in too much pot smoke or something, or did the guy go, "The fook you doing?"

Keith with an Irish accent? What the fook? That couldn't be right. But, yeah, probably being in Dublin, the Keifer figured to go native.

The guy was going, "The fecking cigarette has burned me lip."

Slide nearly said, *You're half in the bag*. Instead, let the crowbar do the talking—walloped the fuck on the head and that's all she wrote. He bundled the guy over his shoulder—the guy weighed, what, seven stone?—and started away, when the side door opened again.

"Ar, bollix," Slide muttered as he ducked with Keifer

behind some leaking bags of garbage and almost passed out from the stench. Not of the rubbish—of Keifer. How much cologne was the dude wearing? Did all rock stars drench themselves in that shite? Even through the sack the guy reeked to bloody high heaven. No wonder Mick got all the babes.

The door opened and closed—the coast was clear. He didn't see anyone else till, at the top of the alley, a bouncer looked over.

Slide said, "Garbage run." To hear the music papers tell it, the Stones had been rubbish for the last decade, right?

Slide thought he was fooked, but the bouncer was distracted by the arrival of a white limo. Slide slipped past him, moving towards his car, parked on Nassau Street.

He threw the guy in the front seat, buckled him in, and burned rubber outa there.

Outside the city limits, he pulled into a lay by. He wanted to see the famous guitarist up close. But then, pulling the sack off the man's head, he echoed his favorite words of James Joyce, going "Aw shite...shite and onions."

Whoever this guy was, he wasn't Keith Richards. He was in his fifties, thick lips, with a scar to the right of his mouth, a button nose and blue eyes. The guy had to be fooking Irish.

The guy came to, seemed completely lost for a while. Then he focused, looked at Slide, and asked, "What the hell is going on?"

Slide nearly whined, "You're not Keith Richards?"

The guy gave a laugh, no humor in it, a sound that seemed to reflect a life where shite happened often and always.

The guy went, "Don't you know me?"

Slide didn't, said, "I don't."

The guy sighed, as in *Give me patience Lord*, then said, "I'm a crime writer."

"A what?"

"A crime writer. I've won the Macavity for—"

Slide shut him off, roared, "Ary Christ, shut the fook up or I'll remove all your fookin' cavities and your tonsils too! Are you somebody? Anyone give a damn about you?"

The guy looked crestfallen, stammered, "I-I got starred reviews in *Publishers Weekly* and *Booklist*... well, maybe I caught them on an off day b-but—"

Slide gave him a slap in the mouth, said, "I don't want to hear about your bloody career. I want to hear somebody will pay cash, lots of cash to have you back."

The guy rubbed his face—poor fuck looked like he'd been beaten and hard, many times—and went, "Maybe my agent...." The bastard paused, reached in his jacket and took out a pack of Major and the Zippo. He lit up and asked, "Got any Jameson?"

Slide was suddenly thrown into that total rage that sometimes just snuck up on him. He said, "Shut the fuck up. I need to think and I need you to shut the hell up, can you do that?"

The writer couldn't. Began to list the titles of his

books and how he'd once been nominated for an Oscar, or Edgar, or some other odd name, and how the U.K. had a hard-on for him.

Slide said, "I'm gonna let it slide, hear?"

But a moment later he had the crowbar in his hand and was beating the bejaysus outa him.

The thin fook was going, "I wrote a book with another guy. Maybe he can—"

But he never got to finish as Slide lashed the crowbar into his teeth, then took out the bastard's left eye with an almighty swing. "Keep yer eye on the main chance," he muttered.

Then Slide looked up to see a family in a nearby car, looking on in horror.

Slide panicked. He opened the door, kicked the body out, and went, "That should sell some books." Then he drove off like your proverbial bat out of hell.

Looking in the rearview, with the pedal to the floor, Slide knew one thing—the kidnapping biz in Ireland had gone bust. He and Angela were going to have to get the fook out of the country, and fast.

Nine

Felicia didn't know how much more Max Fisher she could take. Lettting him touch her—shit, that was the easy part—it was everything else about the man that was driving her crazy.

At first she thought it was gonna be easy. She was sick of dancing anyway, was looking into doing something else. Thought maybe she'd be an escort. She'd do it high end cause, damn, she knew girls didn't have half her ass making a thousand a night. Or maybe she'd get back into pornos. She used to do that shit, back in the nineties. But she was thirty-six now and knew if she tried to get back into films them fat white-ass producer motherfuckers with the cigars hanging in their mouths like big-ass dicks would tell her she was too old, too fat, too this, too that. She'd want to say to them, Look who's talking about fat, bunch of hairy, sweatin', beer-gut assholes can't even bend down to tie their own damn shoelaces. Then they'd be going on, telling her her tits were hangin' too low and she needed more surgery. Yeah, like 44 double-E's wasn't enough. Shit. So then, after she went on, got all her surgery, lost the damn weight, she'd have to give 'em blow jobs, maybe fuck 'em too. Then maybe they'd say, "Sorry, baby, you ain't what we lookin' for." Or, if she got *lucky*, they'd give her a role. Yeah, but not in the good movies, like the ones Jenna Jameson gets in. No, she'd have to bust her ass, doing the "mature" movies—you know, the ones with words like "old lady" and "granny" in the titles. She'd be lucky if she got five hundred a film and how was she supposed to pay her rent and all her damn bills with that bullshit?

So this was where her mind was at when Max Fisher walked into the club and asked for a dance. She remembered Fisher—this practically bald-headed white-ass businessman in a suit, acted like he was all that and shit. Did something with computers, always talking about it like it was some hot shit she gave a damn about. Dropping big-ass computer words, like he thought he was Billionaire Gates or something. She used to play along, suck up to him, tell him how smart and cute he was, when really she thought he was as dumb and asshole-ugly as all the rest of 'em. Stuck-up motherfucker always talkin' the way he did about his Porsche and his town house and how much money he had, all that trying-to-impress-her bullshit when the truth was all she cared about was the next twenty-dollar bill he was gonna stick in her panties.

Another thing about Fisher—he was a titty man. When she was doing a dance he didn't look at nothing else but her titties. It was like that was all she was—two titties, and it was like her nipples were made of metal and there were little round magnets in his eyeballs. Too bad he wasn't making the porno movies because her tits were fine enough for him.

Then, one day, she saw something about him in the paper, how he was mixed up in some shootings or whatever. The cops even came to talk to her, wanted to know where he was the night his wife or girlfriend or somebody got shot. She was surprised, never thought a man like that would ever get involved in something like shooting people. Thought he was all bullshit, no action. Finally the man'd done something impressed her.

But after that, she didn't hear nothing about him for a long time. He didn't come into the club no more and she forgot all about him. Then, there he was, back in his seat, asking for a dance. While she was going at it, he asked her if she wanted to be his live-in ho, paying her double what she was making dancing. She thought maybe it wouldn't be such a bad idea. She get to rest her feet and it was better than regular hoin', goin' man to man. And shit, it was lot better than having to suck off some scumbag movie producer for a role in *Horny Grandmas 11*. She'd get to live in a penthouse on the Upper Rich Side, eat as much sushi as she wanted. Ain't nothin' wrong with that shit, right?

What she didn't know, she was getting in with a crazy damn crack dealer.

Man was on the rock all the time. He said it was just balancing him out or some shit, cause of all the drinks he be having, but Felicia knew that was bullshit talking—the man was just a big stupid-ass crackhead who didn't know how to keep his damn mouth shut. Talking like Al

Pacino, thinking he knows shit about hip-hop, and calling her bee-atch all the time. Or how about he's calling people nigger around her, dissing her race and shit? Motherfucka was lucky he was paying her or he woulda wound up with six in his back real quick.

And how many times was the man gonna say chill? Sometimes, listening to him, Felicia would think, does he know how stupid he sounds? And how about the way he treated her, giving her orders, making her walk around topless all the time so he can always be looking at her titties? And, shit, she had to give him lap dances and blow jobs whenever he wanted them. Yeah, he was paying her, but treating her like she was a damn sex slave was bullshit. Crack-smoking dumb-ass motherfucker had no respect for women and shit.

Sometimes he took her out—yeah, like she was a dog that needed walking. Meanwhile, she knew it was only cause he wanted to show her booty off to the whole damn world. Sometime he'd take her to restaurants and clubbing—damn, somebody had to give that man some dancin' lessons—but his favorite place to go was that swimming pool near Times Square. In the middle of the day, he'd make her get in the damn water with him, so he could be sipping on his drinks with the little umbrellas inside them, showing off her booty for all the white-ass businesspeople looking in.

Shit, being around that asshole twenty-four-seven sure as shit wasn't worth the four grand a week he was paying her. Actually, she was making more than that, because she was screwing Katsu, the man's sushi chef, on the side. Yeah, like sometimes when Max was asleep, she'd go into Katsu's room, be on his body, and then she'd go back to Max. One time he went, "How come you smell like fish?" and she thought she'd got busted. She told him she was hungry and went to have a tuna sandwich in the kitchen and the stupid-ass believed her.

She was also making some money going in Max's safe. One time Max was so shit-ass wasted he gave her the combination, so she was going in, taking fifty, a hundred bucks, figuring the man was so high he wasn't gonna keep count.

The money was good but, no, it wasn't worth being around Max, twenty-four-seven.

She was all set to quit—go back to dancing or whatever—when one day Max sent her out to buy some Cuban cigars and a white guy in an ugly-ass plaid suit—shit went out of style in 1974—came up to her and went, "Hey, Felicia."

Just like that, like they was old friends and shit. She never seen him before in her whole damn life but, shit, all you had to do was look at that motherfucker and know he was a cop.

Pretending she didn't know what was going down, she went, "What the fuck you want?"

And then he laid the shit on her straight up. His name was Detective Joe Miscali, NYPD, and he was gonna bust her ass hard for prostitution, possession, whole mess of charges, if she didn't give him some shit on Max Fisher.

She was like, "Shit about what? I don't know shit about nothing."

Playing hardball with the cop, waiting to see if he was for real or not.

Turned out the motherfucker wasn't playing. Said he was on to Max, was ready to take his ass down hard, and he gave her two choices—cooperate or go away. Shit, she didn't want to do no jail, so she said, Yeah, she'd help. What the fuck? She didn't like helping cops, but she'd love to see Max go down, give the old bald-headed bitch some payback for the way he been treating her.

She started trying hard as she could to get Miscali some shit on Max. She was listening in on conversations, trying to always be by him all the time, whatever. Then, one night, he came into the shower, pointing the gun in her face. She thought, *Fuck, he musta found out I'm gonna snitch on his ass*. Then it turned out it wasn't about that at all; it was about the stupid money from the safe. Played it right, denying all the shit he was saying to her, and he finally left her alone.

Later, she heard him talking to his boy Kyle on the phone about some drug deal was gonna go down with some Colombians. He told her to get out of the room, but she was listening in on the call on the other line in the bedroom. Okay, so now she had the info for Joe Miscali and she could stop being Max Fisher's ho— praise the Lord.

But then she got to thinking—a drug deal, and didn't they say it was twenty thousand dollars? There was gonna be product there too and she was thinking, *Why I gotta tell that shit to Miscali?* Felicia been thinking about getting away, leaving New York. She was tired of ho'in, being worried about money all the time. She had her friend Ramona in St. Louis, was always calling her, saying they should open a beauty salon together. But she need money to do that and no bank was gonna start giving no stripper no loan. But maybe if she could figure out a way to get that twenty grand she could go half with Ramona on the salon, get a whole new life started.

Shit, she barely slept the whole night because she was thinking about one thing—how to get that old stinkin' crackhead's money. Then it came to her—her cousin Sha-Sha from Brooklyn. Damn, why didn't she think of that shit straight up?

Sha-Sha was her second cousin on her mom's side. Felicia was six years older than him and funny shit was he was the first trick she ever turned. Happened when she was nineteen and he was thirteen. He was just hitting puberty and he was a horny little thang—nasty too. He was always walking around, touching his dick, asking her to do shit with him. Finally, sick of hearing him talk, she went, "You wanna fuck, I'll fuck, but it's gonna cost you five bucks." He must've gone and stole five bucks from his momma, Felicia's aunt. Was the fastest five dollars she made her whole life.

Felicia told Max she needed to go get a haircut. Meanwhile, she was really going to meet Sha-Sha in Brooklyn, in Canarsie. She took the L train out there and maybe she should've worn some different clothes. In this short leather skirt Max had bought her every guy on the train was wanting to bone her.

Sha-Sha was living in Breukelen Houses, off the L train. It had been a long time since Felicia had been back to the projects and she wasn't missing none of it. When Sha-Sha answered the door she didn't even recognize the nigga. She went, "Sha-Sha here?" and he went, "The fuck you talkin' 'bout?" Yeah, that sounded like Sha-Sha, but what happened to his body? He used to be fine looking—well not too fine, he wasn't no Denzel—but he was big and strong and his face wasn't too bad either. But now the man was fat. She was talking Rerun fat, like the man be eating ten meals a day.

She looked around at all the pizza boxes, Chinese containers and shit and said, "Damn, how much you be eatin'?"

Sha-Sha went, "That how you say hello? How'd you get so rude, bitch?"

"Fuck you," Felicia snapped. After listening to Max call her bee-atch all the time she wasn't gonna take that shit from her damn cousin.

"Sorry, baby," Sha-Sha said smiling. "Come to me."

He held open his arms for a hug but, damn, Felicia felt like she was only getting her arms around one-quarter his body. She was glad she wasn't hookin' no more, havin' Sha-Sha-size men on her body. Nigga that big fall on a girl's body he kill her and shit.

Then Felicia felt one of Sha-Sha's hands grabbing her ass and she shooed it away.

"Don't be grabbin' my ass," she said.

"Shit, you lookin' good," Sha-Sha said. "Smellin' good too. I bet you nice and tasty."

Listen to the nigga, talkin' to her like she was food. She better watch out—the fat motherfucka might eat her.

When he started kissing her neck—sucking on it more like it—she pushed him away. Tried to push him away. Nigga didn't budge.

"The fuck you doin'?" Felicia said. "Ain't you forgettin' we cousins?"

"Shit never stopped you before," Sha-Sha said.

Sha-Sha grabbed her ass again. She slapped his hand hard and went, "I ain't playin'," and he finally let go.

He moved some pizza boxes off the couch and they sat down, got caught up and shit. He asked her if she was still dancing and she said "Yeah," leaving out that she was Max Fisher's ho. Then she asked him if he was still dealing and he said, "Yeah," and she was thinking, *I wonder what shit he's leaving out.*

Felicia didn't want to spend her whole damn day bullshitting in the projects. Yeah, Max was a bitch-ass motherfucker, but living in a penthouse—shit, she could get used to that. So getting right down to it, she went, "Yo, there's this white motherfucker I know. You know, I dance for him and shit. Motherfucker's dealing rock."

"Who's he with?" Sha-Sha asked.

"Ain't with nobody," Felicia said. "See how stupid his ass is? He don't even know he keep it up the gangs're gonna be coming down on his ass. His clients—yeah, motherfucker calls 'em *clients,* are all rich-ass white people like he is. Nigga's gettin' all the white people in Manhattan smokin' rock and shit."

"Damn," Sha-Sha said smiling.

"So I be thinking," Felicia said. "Why wait till the

gangs come down on him, know what I'm sayin'? How 'bout I find some way to get down on his ass first?"

"Shit makes sense," Sha-Sha said.

"Shit makes lotta sense," Felicia said. "So nigga's on the phone last night, talkin' about this deal's gonna go down with these Colombians, for twenty thousand dollars and shit. Then I think about you and your boys and I'm like, 'Yeah, we can get in on that shit.' Know what I'm saying?"

Sha-Sha was into a pack of Chips Ahoy, eating the shit two at time. Piling that shit down his throat like his damn life depended on it.

"Shit, you eatin' or listenin'?" Felicia asked.

Sha-Sha gave her a long look, swallowing cookies, then said, "Keep talkin' to me."

"What I been saying," Felicia said. "All I gotta do is find out where the drug deal's at, right? Then you and your boys, whatever, bust in on that shit, know what I'm sayin'? I get the money, you get the rock. Shit, Max—that's the nigga's name—payin' twenty for it, shit's gotta be worth forty, right? You know how much pizza and cookies and Pringles and whatever the fuck else you been eatin' make you so damn fat you can buy for forty thousand dollars?...A lot, that's how much."

Sha-Sha thought it over for a few seconds, stuffing more cookies down his mouth—looked like he was swallowing them whole—then went, "Max huh? And you say the nigga don't got no back-up?"

"Ain't you listenin' to me?" Felicia said. "It's just him, he's alone. Oh, yeah, and some white boy from Alabama. Name Kyle or some shit. Max and Kyle.

That sounds like two scary-ass motherfuckers, right?"

Felicia laughed.

Sha-Sha wasn't laughing, went, "What about them Colombians?"

"What about 'em?"

"You say this is twenty thousand dollar, right? Shit, ain't no high-level deal for no twenty thousand dollars, know what I'm sayin'? Sound like some street-level bullshit to me."

"Yeah, yeah, I know. So? That makes the whole thing even more easy. How hard's it gonna be for you and whoever else you got backin' you up, do whatever you gotta do. Shit gonna be stupid easy, you ask me."

"Yeah, I guess maybe I can get my boy Troit in on it with me," Sha-Sha said. "We split up the rock together and shit."

"That's right," Felicia said, "and I get the money. That's all I want—the twenty grand. I don't care if they got a hundred grand worth of rock there. All I want is the cash."

She liked the deal, but she didn't like the sound of Troit. If he was in with Sha-Sha, he was probably some sick-ass, that was for damn sure.

Sha-Sha was quiet a few seconds, like he was thinking real hard, then said, "You know I might gotta cap this Max motherfucker, right?"

"Shit, you wanna cap him, go 'head," Felicia said. "You be doin' me a favor, wanna know the truth. Cap his ass in the head, serve him right for the way he been treatin' me. Walking around with my titties showin' all the time, makin' me do him whenever he get a hard-on, which is like what, five, six, seven times a day? Man's little dick be hard all the time with all the Vi-agra he be takin'."

"A'ight, I'm in, yo," Sha-Sha said. "Let's bust this Max nigga hard." Then he pushed the Chips Ahoys aside, said, "Man, I'm gettin' sick off these cookies. Man need some real dessert, know what I'm sayin'?"

Felicia smiled, like she didn't know what Sha-Sha was saying, and said, "Yo, I should be gettin' back. I don't want Max getting' suspicious or nothin'. I told him I was gonna get a haircut but it ain't gonna be no shorter when I get back. Not like his cracked-up ass would notice."

As Felicia headed toward the door Sha-Sha said, "You think I'm playin' with you?"

Felicia stopped, looked back at him. He had his legs spread and he was undoing the buckle on his belt.

"Come on, Sha-Sha, don't be doing that shit. We cousins."

"You want me to do shit for you, you better do some shit for me. Know what I'm saying?"

Felicia knew she had no choice. Shit would end fast anyway. Besides, had to be better than Max, right?

When she had her panties down and was climbing on she went, "You better be quick. And you tell our mommas about this shit, I'll kill you."

When Felicia was done screwin' Sha-Sha she took the train back to Manhattan. Man, it was a relief being back in Manhattan, being back in *the city*. She was through with all that being in Brooklyn, back in the projects bullshit. She had class now and she wasn't gonna be poor ever again. All she needed was the time and place of the meeting with the Colombians and Sha-Sha would take care of all the rest. She'd have her money, be able to open her salon in St. Louis, her life would be all set up.

That night, when she was in bed with Max, she figured there was no use not getting right to it and she said, "When's the drug meeting with the Colombians at?"

She figured Max would just come out and tell her. Why'd he have to keep it a secret?

But either he thought something was up or he was just being an asshole, cause he said, "Why the fuck do you care?"

Shit, why'd she have to be so straight up with him? She shoulda tried to work it out of him, or waited till they were in the swimming pool at the QT and he was in a good mood and shit.

"No reason," Felicia said, twirling her finger in his sweaty gray chest hair, acting all lovey dovey with the damn asshole. "I just wanna know where my man's gonna be at, that's all."

"Hey, let's not forget your role in this relationship," Max said. "I'm not your man, I'm your boss. You got that?"

Damn, she wanted to bitch slap his ass.

"Yeah, I got it," she said. "But ain't I gonna come with you to meet the Colombians?"

Max laughed then said, "Honey, this is business, complicated stuff. Your role is to be waiting for me when I get back. I'm gonna be very worked up after that meeting and I'm gonna to need my bee-atch to relax me. Now make yourself useful and roll me a joint, will ya?"

She knew it was because he'd caught—well, almost caught—her going into the safe. Now he wasn't gonna trust her with nothing.

In the morning she was ready to give up, say fuck you to the whole busting in on the drug deal idea. She was gonna call Detective Miscali and give him whatever he wanted and then she was gonna get her ass outa, what'd he call it? Oh, yeah, *FisherLand*.

But then the next morning Max's boy Kyle arrived up from Alabama. One look at that white boy and Felicia knew she was back in action. When she first saw him she even said out loud, "Damn, that boy be white."

Serious, if there ever was a white boy, it was Kyle. Damn, nigga put the white in white boy. She didn't know how he was from the South because his skin looked like he was one of them albinos, like he hadn't been out in the sun his whole hillbilly life. Probably because he spent all his time in church, that's why. The boy be carrying around his bible all the time, talking to Max about crack—how fucked up is that? Max had told her something about how he was gonna set Kyle up with some ho's when he came to the city, wanted to know if Felicia had any "references," but Felicia knew the only ho on that boy's body was gonna be her.

And she could tell the boy was hard up, looked like a dog that wasn't getting none. Whenever he looked at her his mouth hung open, like he couldn't believe what he was seeing. She kept him in heat, brushing her titties up against his arm, touching his ass with her index finger, and all the time she kept thinking, "She-itt, this boy be white."

And the way he talked, like some southern gent and calling her "Ma'am." Ain't nobody ever called Felicia ma'am and she had to be real careful not to laugh in his damn fool face.

But, shit, she kind of liked the way he was worshipping her, treating her with her respect. Aretha said it right—ain't no girl on the planet gonna turn down some r-e-s-p-e-c-t. And, hell, being called ma'am was better than being called bee-atch, right?

One time, in the kitchen, she moved up close to him, her titties right up against his chest, and tried getting the drug deal info from him but he clammed way up, stuttering, "I-I-I don't think the The M.A.X. w-w-would like me talking 'bout that, m-m-m-a'am."

Stuttering and shit, he was so nervous. She wanted to slap him upside his head, get some sense in his dumb Southern boy ass, but then she needed that information. There was only one way she knew she could get it out of him—fuckin'. There wasn't a man alive didn't talk like a jackrabbit when he got some pussy with the promise of more to come. Besides, she was screwing her own damn cousin, what was one more little white boy?

Later that day, Max went out to sell some of his crack to somebody and Katsu was out buying fish in Chinatown. Felicia put on some of the lingerie Max had got her and went out into the living room. Kyle was sitting on the couch and when he looked up at her he almost dropped his damn bible. She didn't say nothing, just looked him up and down and then went to the stereo and put on some Mary J. Blige. Then she got a bottle of bourbon, two glasses, piled some ice in there and then splashed lots of booze in each. Holding the glasses in one hand, like she'd seen in a movie, she strolled across the room to where Kyle was now sitting straight up, like he was an army man, and went, "Girl sure does hate to drink alone, suga."

He took the glass, his hand shaking, and she eased down next to him. He gulped the bourbon straight down, swallowed the ice too, like he needed it to cool off.

Squeezing up nice and close to him, she went, "What you readin'?"

Kyle could barely speak, he wanted it so bad. He went, "E-E-Ezekiel eigh-eighteen twenty-seven."

"Ooh, that sounds nice," Felicia said, puckering up her lips. "What it say?"

"N-nothing much, ma'am," Kyle said. "Just that, um, uh, 'When the wicked man turneth away from his wickedness that he hath committed, and doeth that which is lawful and right, he shall save his soul alive.' "

"Oh, yeah, that sounds real pretty," Felicia rubbed his leg—damn, he had a tent in his sweatpants already—then went, "You know, I go to church all the time too?"

"Really?"

She wanted to laugh in his face, but she had to keep this shit going.

"Yeah, I always sit up close, in the first row, so I can

hear what the reverend say loud and clear. You know, I'm related to Dr. Martin Luther King?"

Damn, she wished she could take that shit back. Boy was from the south, might be some kind of racist or something.

But, nope, turned out it was the perfect way to go because he went, "Wow, Dr. King, that's real impressive, ma'am. I'm a big, big fan. How're you and the Reverend related?"

Shit—questions. She wasn't expecting that.

"He was my mom's cousin twice removed on my sister's side. But he and my mom was real close—like brothers. I mean brother and sister." Figuring she had to get off this subject real quick, she went, "You know what I like about you?" She was tickling his leg a little, happy to see that big tent coming up already in his pants—yeah, boy was ready to go campin' all right. "You real polite, that's what. Callin' me ma'am all the time. I like that shit. Wanna know something else? You real pretty too."

She almost said *purty*, but figured they were past that.

She grabbed the bible from him, tossed it onto the floor, and climbed on his body.

"Don't worry none about your bible, honey chile. We can have our own, private bible class. I be Eve, you be Adam, and our asses are stuck in the Garden of Eden."

"O-okay, ma'am," he said. He could barely talk. Shit, he could barely breathe.

She grinded up against him, putting his face right

between her titties, then said, "Ain't there a snake in the garden of Eden?" and undid the snap on his Levi's.

"H-hold up a second, ma'am," Kyle said. "Ain't you Max's...I mean The M.A.X.'s girl?"

"Honey, I ain't nobody's girl," Felicia said.

She got his pants down, then pulled his shirt up over his head. Then she took his Y-fronts down and she couldn't believe what she was seeing.

She went, "Damn, boy, you are *hung*."

And she wasn't lying neither, like when she told all them pencil dicks that they got the biggest cocks she ever seen just to boost their egos and shit. Sometimes she even told Max he had a big one. Meanwhile, sometimes she couldn't even feel the shit. He'd roll off her and go, "I'm done," and she didn't even know they was started yet.

But, Kyle, man, he was the real deal. She'd been with half the Knicks and most of the brothers in Canarsie and, shit, none of them had nothing on this white boy.

"Thank you, ma'am," he said.

"Naw, thank *you*," she said, and they got at it. She didn't want him to shoot too soon, because those southern boys—even the gents like Kyle—turned real mean when that happened.

Felicia was letting loose, coming like the goddamn D-train, shrieking like a crack ho who'd had her shit taken away.

Meanwhile, Kyle was going, "Am I hurting you, ma'am?"

She just screamed at him, "You da man, you da man, you da man!"

When she finished up she turned over and let Kyle do his thing. When he blew he didn't make a sound. Boy was too polite to make noise.

Sitting up on the couch after, Felicia went, "I ain't been fucked like that in a long, long time, suga."

Then she saw he was crying, big-ass tears going down his cheeks.

"What's the matter, baby?"

He could hardly talk, he was crying so bad.

Then he went, "I've betrayed The M.A.X. What am I gonna do now?"

Boy was so messed up he didn't even remember to call her ma'am.

She caressed his cheek, went, "Ain't no power on earth can stop love, honey."

"You really mean that? You…l-l-love me?"

"Why you think I'm here with you right now, baby? I ain't usually the type of girl who gets with a man real quick, know what I'm sayin'?"

Lucky she wasn't Pinnochio or her nose'd be blowing a hole through the door, past the elevators, out the damn building and shit.

Kyle said, "But The M.A.X. said that you're a…a… a ho."

"That's bullshit," Felicia said. "Don't listen to anything Max be saying to you cause that man got his head inside his ass, know what I'm sayin'? I ain't no ho. I'm just a woman, a lonely woman lookin' for love, and now I found it."

She saw his eyes well up and let him kiss her, trying not to laugh, then said, "You love me, too, don't you? I can see you do. I can see it. And listen, baby, if you love somebody, you tell them everything. There ain't no secrets. So why don't you tell me where that drug deal's gonna be at?"

"Can I ask why you want to know?"

She wanted to go, "No, you can't," but went with, "Cause I just like to know where my man be at, that's all….You are my man, ain't you?"

She saw the way he was looking at her and that was it, piece of cake. He told her everything she wanted to know about the drug deal—the time, the place, who was gonna be there, everything.

Then he said, all scared and shit, "You sure you won't tell The M.A.X., ma'am? I mean, I know it's no big deal and all, but I don't think The M.A.X. would appreciate it if he knew I told you something I wasn't supposed to."

Yeah, Kyle had a big dick but Felicia had never seen a pussy like him her whole damn life. Never saw a sucker like him neither.

"Don't worry," she said. "Be our own little secret." Then she climbed back on him and she said, "You like Britney?" Kyle said yeah and she said, "Then what you waitin' for? Hit me one more time, baby."

Ten

Sideswipe
CHARLES WILLEFORD

Joe Miscali was a good guy. You ask anyone and they'd go, "Joe? Yeah, he's a good guy." It seemed like everybody loved Joe and you had to wonder—where's the flaw? what's wrong with this picture?—since Joe was a cop and, yeah, a damn good one.

He'd worked out of the 19th Precent so long that they called him Joe Nineteen. Even the bad guys kinda had a soft spot for Joey Nineteen. He was divorced—sure, came with the doughnuts and the buzz haircut—but even his ex old lady had nothing but nice things to say about him. She'd go, *Joe? Oh, yeah, Joe, he's a good guy.*

Joe didn't work at being Mr. Nice. He was just one of those rarities, a good man in a bad situation.

He was built like a brick shithouse—pug face, broken-veined complexion, hands thick as shovels. A typical Joe Miscali outfit: polyester pants with a nylon shirt and a plaid sports coat. Note to Norman Mailer: *Good guys wear plaid.* He was born in Queens, loved the Mets, Jets and Nets. He watched re-runs of *The Odd Couple*, like, a lot. He loved to quote from the show, insert lines into casual conversation even if no one understood what the hell he was talking about. Silly, yeah, but Joe got a kick out of it.

His lineage was that old volatile mix of Italian and mick. So how'd he wind up with such a sunny disposition? Go figure.

Joe had a pretty good record of closing cases. Not that he was a great cop but he was smart, knew snitches were the way to go. He'd been lucky, often getting to the right snitch at the right time. Thing is, like luck, snitches had a very short shelf life, so you got as much as you could from them before their mouths or dope took them off the board.

If there was a sadness in Joe's life, it was for Kenneth Simmons, an old buddy from way back. They'd gone to the Academy together and the son of a bitch had been a hell of a cop—relentless, never let go. Joe admired that, but it would turn out to be Kenny's downfall. Last year, he was after Max Fisher, a smarmy, smug businessman who was on the hook for killing his wife and another woman. Over brews one night, Kenny'd told Joe, "The schmuck is guilty and I'm gonna nail him."

But someone'd nailed Ken before the case got up and running, and no one had ever really gone down for it. Joe kept an eye on the Fisher punk, knowing that somehow, in some goddamned way, he'd been the cause of Kenneth's death.

Kenneth had had a partner, a cocky mother named Ortiz. Joe could never figure the deal out—Kenneth, a sweetheart and Oritz, a badged prick. But, hey, like marriage, you never knew what glued people together.

After Kenneth bought the farm, Ortiz had let the case go. Time to time, Joe would ask him if anything was breaking on the deal, but it seemed like Ortiz had given up. Then, one night, Ortiz was killed instantly in a smash-up on the Jersey Turnpike on his way to A.C. to—rumor had it—screw some bimbo he had down there. And this with a wife, eight months pregnant, home in his apartment in the Bronx. Nice guy, huh? What was left of Ortiz they shoveled back to some small town in Santa Domingo.

Joe kept an eye on Max, hoping to get some closure for Ken. Yeah, it had become personal to Joe. There was sure some weird karma around that Fisher fuck, like everyone round him got wiped and he just kept on keeping on.

Then Fisher went off the radar. Joe heard he'd fallen on hard times, gone broke somehow, was drinking his ass off, got into a couple of bar fights. Did Joe shed any tears? Like fuck he did. He was secretly hoping that Max would piss the wrong guy off at some bar, get his ass nailed to the wall.

A couple months went by and Joe didn't hear much of anything. Then imagine how surprised he was when he heard that Fisher was back and, word was, he was dealing. You fucking believe it?

Joe put a tag on Max. Yeah, he could've nailed him for a couple of small-time crack deals, could have at least slapped him with Possession with Intent. But the DA wanted the whole deal and didn't want Joe to move in too quick. So Joe got a hold of a new snitch— a stripper-slash-prostitute named Felicia Howard. No surprise there—Fisher was as smarmy as they came and he had a thing for busty broads. Fisher's old flame, Angela Petrakos, had also been built.

Felicia was promising—Joe had scared her and good. He had her on prostitution charges for taking money from the clients she danced for and was hanging three-to-five, no parole, over her head. He could tell she was probably sick of Fisher herself. There was no way in hell she'd go down for that jackass.

The early stages with a snitch were always tricky. He had to build up trust, or if not trust, at least a relationship. He never had any problem with paying his informants. Some cops, they used intimidation, bullied the poor fucks into giving up information but Joe knew that way you only got half the story. First thing Joe did, always, was slip them a few bucks and it worked every time. Nothing like cash money to loosen up somebody's lips. And paying hookers for info usually worked out really well. If they'd give away their bodies for some green, why wouldn't they give up info?'

But Joe had been working with Felicia for over a week now and he was getting impatient. He felt like she was stalling.

He arranged to meet her at the Green Kitchen diner on Seventy-seventh and First. They did some mean meatloaf there, not a bad rice pudding either. When Joe was seated at a booth toward the back he spotted a dog-eared paperback with a torn cover that somebody had left on the cushion. He could barely read the title—was it *Cockfighter?*

Whatever, he thought, and shoved it aside.

Felicia arrived. It was hard not to notice her in the short skirt and with all the cleavage. Practically every male head in the diner turned to watch her pass. A few women too. When she sat across from Joe, he smiled. He gave great smile. Ask anybody.

He gave Felicia that look, then went, "You need anything?" and took out his wallet, showing her the corner of a twenty sticking out. Figuring he'd whet her appetite right off the bat.

"Why you so good to me, Detective Miscali?" Felicia said. "I ain't used to kindness."

He knew she was full of shit, went, "You're full of shit." And yeah, here was his handkerchief, all sympathy and bull, and he said, "Felicia, I'm your friend, I'm gonna get those minor charges wiped but you gotta give me something on Fisher, you know, keep my bosses happy. And call me Joe, okay?"

She nodded, wiping daintily at her eyes, and said, hesitantly, "Maybe I do got something for you…Joe."

He was all focus now, cop antennae on full alert. Asked, "What is it?"

"Hold up," she said. "What am I gonna get?"

"You get not to go to jail."

"I mean what am I gonna get's green and white, has presidents on 'em."

"Look, Felicia," Joe said. "Just because I haven't played hardball with you yet, doesn't mean I'm not capable. Yeah, I'm a good guy, but I have a hardass side to me, too, and, trust me, you don't want to meet it."

Joe was trying to intimidate. He knew it wasn't working—hell, she knew he knew it wasn't working—but he kept the glare going anyway.

She nodded, said, "I'm just playin' with you. You know how bad I wanna help you, right? But I just hope there's more twenties like that in yo' wallet, know what I'm sayin'?"

"How many twenties we talking about?" Joe said, smiling.

"Fifty," Felicia said.

The smile went. Joe said. "Look, if you think I'm giving you a thousand bucks you're out of your fucking mind."

"Five hundred," Felicia said.

"Two hundred," Joe said.

"Deal," Felicia said.

Joe, feeling like he'd been taken, went, "Do you have anything for me or not?"

"Yeah, I got somethin' good for you," Felicia said. "You gonna be thankin' me for this shit. He's in with some Colombians."

Joe waited a second then said, "You mean Colombian Colombians. *From* Colombia."

"Ain't talkin' about no District of Columbians," Felicia said. "He's movin' up—way up. Motherfuckers are from some drug cartel or some shit. They having a big meeting in Staten Island tomorrow night. You show up there, you can get 'em all."

Felicia gave Joe all the info about the meeting and Joe didn't think she was bullshitting. When you worked with snitches you had to have a good bullshit detector, and Joe had one of the best in the business. He wrote everything in his pad, meticulous to get every detail down. After a few minutes or so of this, he looked up at Felicia and said, "Can I ask where you got this?"

"How you know Max didn't tell me?"

Joe gave her a look, like, Was I born yesterday?

Felicia recognized the look, went, "From Kyle, some white boy from Alabama. The boy's hung, know what I'm saying?"

Joe smiled at his snitch, proud of how well everything had worked out.

"Nice work," he said. Then he grabbed a menu and went, "Now how about we get some food on the table, you hungry girl you."

Eleven

Burn
Sean Doolittle

Angela was fuming, not from the cigs she was chain smoking but from waiting for Slide again. *Where the fook was he?* He'd said he was going to kidnap the Rolling Stones. It seemed like a great idea at the time, but only because she'd been three sheets to the Jameson wind. Yeah, bring back the Stones, way to go, Slide, good on yah. Bloody Jameson, it was worse than any drug. Not only did it tell you you could do anything, it downright persuaded you that the maddest, most insane scenario would work. How else can you explain Riverdance?

But he seemed gung ho on the idea and she knew men well enough to let them do all kinds of crazy shite and then she'd reap the reward. She heard the car pull up and then Slide was running towards the house—alone. What, no Jagger? No Richards? Not even Charlie Fookin' Watts?

Slide came bursting in, going, "Gotta have me big drink."

She wondered what happened to, *And how was your day, sweetheart?* Fucking men—me, me, me. But she got a glass, poured a large Jameson, then asked in a cold tone, "Ice with that, sweetheart?"

Get Hard Case Crime by Mail...
And Save 43%!

☐ YES! Sign me up for the Hard Case Crime Book Club!

As long as I choose to stay in the club, I will receive every Hard Case Crime book as it is published (generally one each month). I'll get to preview each title for 10 days. If I decide to keep it, I will pay only $3.99* — a savings of 43% off the cover price! There is no minimum number of books I must buy and I may cancel my membership at any time.

Name: _____

Address: _____

City / State / ZIP: _____

Telephone: _____

E-Mail: _____

☐ **I want to pay by credit card:** ☐ VISA ☐ MasterCard ☐ Discover

Card #: _____ Exp. date: _____

Signature: _____

Mail this card to:
HARD CASE CRIME BOOK CLUB
1 Mechanic Street, Norwalk, CT 06850-3431

Or fax it to 610-995-9274.
You can also sign up online at www.dorchesterpub.com.

* Plus $2.00 for shipping. Offer open to residents of the U.S. and Canada only. Canadian residents please call 1-800-481-9191 for pricing information.

If you are under 18, a parent or guardian must sign. Terms, prices, and conditions subject to change. Subscription subject to acceptance. Dorchester Publishing reserves the right to reject any order or cancel any subscription.

Leaning on the endearment, like they even had a fucking refrigerator.

Then she noticed Slide was dripping with sweat. And was that blood?

He gulped the drink, belched, said, "Sweet Jaysus." Then he said, "We gotta get out of here, now, and I mean not just outa here but, but outa the country."

She had to know, asked, "What happened?"

The booze seemed to calm him a bit. He took a deep breath, said, "I took the wrong guy, all right? A fookin writer, and turns out he's related to one of the Boyos, you know, the IRA?"

Was he kidding? She knew who they were. More important, she knew you don't, like, ever fuck with them. There wasn't much that scared Angela. Growing up in New Jersey, her friends used to worry about the Mob. Like if Angela picked up some Soprano at a bar her friends would tell her she was crazy, she didn't know what she was getting into. But Angela would just laugh, knowing a Soprano was a kitten compared to a Boyo.

She nearly shrieked, "Are you sure?"

If Slide had really kidnapped one of their relatives, oh Sweet Jesus, that was like fookin' suicide.

Slide gave her the look, said, "No, I'm making it up." Then went, "Of course I'm sure. He even had a Belfast accent and he said they'd cut me balls off."

That convinced her. She knew, alas, that was exactly what they'd do.

She asked, "Did you give him back?"

He seemed stunned, said, "Are you stone mad? It's

not like a pair of jeans that didn't fit, I couldn't *return* him. I didn't, like, keep the receipt. Oh, and here's the worst part."

Christ, what could be worse, unless he killed him? The blood, she realized with a sinking heart.

She said, "You didn't—"

Slide interrupted, went, "I was seen, all right? Well, at least the car was and they got me number, they'll be able to track us in jig time."

She wanted to scream, *Us? You stupid prick, it's you.*

He read her mind, asked in a chilling voice, "You wouldn't run out on me, would you?"

Angela shuddered as the past danced before her eyes. She mostly suppressed her past, kept it locked nice and tight. Like they said on *Seinfeld*, It was in the vault. But sometimes it came out to play.

Her mother had had connections to the Boyos. Time to time, some shadowy figure would arrive, literally off the boat, with that thick Belfast accent and thicker manners. Her mother would feed him and he'd get Angela's room.

One freezing February night, before Angela left home for good, one of these guys arrived. Had that Marine Corps look about him, ramrod straight, shaved head, menace oozing from him.

Angela's mother was at work—she worked with a cleaning crew that serviced the Flatiron Building, supplemented her income by stealing books from a publisher who had offices there and returning them to various bookstores around the city for credit. Angela arrived home to find this guy in the kitchen, dressed in just a string vest and combat trousers and reading *An Poblacht*, some paper Sinn Fein sold in the Irish pubs. Her mother had warned her, severely, *Don't ever, ever talk to these men.*

Like hello. You tell a woman like Angela to stay away from a certain man and, gee, guess what?

Angela was in man-eater attire, the mini, the sheer hose, heels. The *wanna fuck?* jobs. They were killing her, naturally—did men actually believe women enjoyed wearing these things?—and was heading out when he spoke, startling her.

"What's yer hurray, *cailin?*"

He put the paper aside and she saw the gun. He'd taken it apart and was cleaning it. It looked sleek and ugly. He was wearing Doc Martens and used his boot to push a chair aside.

He ordered, "Take a pew."

Mainly, she wanted to take her goddamn heels off but his whole languid lethal attitude was strangely exciting.

He said, "You'll be knowing why I'm here."

She didn't, said, "I don't."

He snapped the barrel of the weapon in one fluid motion and the gun was assembled. He laid it on the table and said, "I've a bit of business in Arizona. A bollix stole from us and I'm going to recover it."

He was smiling, but no warmth or humor came from it. She felt sorry for the poor bastard in Arizona.

"They tell me tis fierce hot out that way," he said, and she said, "Dry heat."

He laughed, more like the sound of an animal's

grunt, and said, "Only in America. Back home, you could say we have wet rain…lashings of it."

She was tempted to say, "How utterly fascinating."

Now he rolled a cigarette, expertly, like Bogart in the old movies, with one hand. He licked the paper and produced a Zippo with a logo on the side, *Fifth of*…something. She couldn't see the rest.

One flick and he was lit. He drew deep, then exhaled right into her face and said,

"Afore I go, I have a wee job to do for yer Mammie."

She knew better than to ask.

He seemed to know she wouldn't and said, "Yer Uncle Billy, he used yer Mammie's name to get a loan and the fooker, he's welshed on the repayment, left her in a right old mess, and old Billy, he supports the English Team."

The latter seemed to be the greater crime, if his expression was any indication. He offered her the cig, the butt wet from his lips, and she was too rattled not to accept.

As she took a full pull he grinned and said, "You like it unfiltered, don't you, gra?" Then he took it back, mashed it on the floor, and went, "I'm going to tell you what's coming down the pike for our Billy, so you know…never…fooking never…piss on the Movement or yer own kind. We never forget and we never fooking forgive, you got that?"

Hard not to.

She nodded slowly, hoping the wetness between her legs didn't show in her face, though she felt a burn on her cheeks.

"First I kneecap him," he explained, "and then, as he called yer mammie a toerag—see, the hoor's ghost is using Brit words—I'll cut off two of his toes and shove them down his gullet. Make him eat his words, and every time he hobbles around, he'll remember…" Then he sat straight up, asked, "Don't you have work to do?"

She tried to stand but her knees were shaking.

He went, "Any chance you could make a fellah a decent cup of tea?"

She never saw him again, though she did see Uncle Billy, with a cane and about twenty added years in his face. She couldn't help wondering if he'd been able to pass the toes, though she imagined that looking in the toilet bowl must have been a fascinating adventure for him from then on.

Now, looking at Slide in horror, she couldn't believe he'd screwed with the lads. Oh sweet Jesus, they'd make him eat both legs—and as for her, she was, in their eyes, one of their own.

She wanted to scream. "You crazy bastard, you've really put your foot in it. Where are we supposed to go?"

"America," Slide said.

And so they sat down, hatched out a plan to get some serious money and fast. In spite of all the fear, all the anger she felt toward Slide, Angela was excited about the thought of returning to New York. Oh God, she realized how much she missed it.

She gave Slide her full look, drilled her eyes into his, and she couldn't help marveling at the piercing blue. His expression, as usual, was impossible to read, though. You never knew if he was planning murder, mayhem and general madness, thinking about sex, or some of each.

"Okay," she said. "Here's what we're going to do and this is how we're going to do it."

The plan: They'd hit the bars, the posh ones where the suits and the money hung. She'd lure some schmuck outside and then Slide would do his gig. She was estimating if they hit maybe ten pubs, they'd score, say, in six, and have the run-like-fook-away money.

Slide was game, said, "Game on."

As long as violence was in the mix, he was up for it.

She cautioned, "And try not to kill anyone, can you fucking do that?"

He smiled, said, "I love it when you talk dirty to me."

Twelve

If a man should challenge me now, I would go to that man
and take him kindly and forgivingly by the hand,
lead him to a quiet retired spot and kill him.
MARK TWAIN

Max was gearing up for the big meeting with the
Colombians, trying to learn as much *Español* as he
could. He'd sent his bee-atch out to get him the tapes
and he was listening to them whenever he had time,
which wasn't often because he was *mucho* busy. *Mucho*,
see how he intuitively knew this shit?

The idea to learn Spanish came to Max one morning
on the bowl when he was thinking because, like,
thinking was his forte.

See, when you were a clued-in dude like The
M.A.X., you not only got to use words like *forte*, you
had a reasonable idea of what they meant. He'd been
telling himself like a mantra, *know your market*, and
know the guys you're dealing with. He hadn't built up
this hell of a business without being savvy, and he liked
to think of himself as straddling both sides. Yeah, the
boardroom, piece of cake, he could do the biz gig in
his sleep. Sometimes he believed he was born with the
Dow Jones in his mouth. Your regular working stiff, he
read the sports section of the *Daily News*, moved his
lips as he read, but The M.A.X., he didn't just read the

business section, he fucking devoured it. *Wall Street Journal*, man, he subscribed, and knew his name was in every editor's address book over there. Come on, if you were a journalist in the business world and didn't have an in with Max Fisher, then who the hell were you anyway?

Who knew, maybe one of these days the *Journal* would ask Max to do a regular column for them and if Max was in a philanthropic mood, had some free time on his hands, felt the need to *give back*, maybe he'd accept. He'd call the column, what else, *The M.A.X.* Have guys in all the happening bars going, "I was reading in *The M.A.X.*..." or "*The M.A.X.* says..." Yeah, he could see it. The double hit of coke he'd had with his croissant and skim milk latte helped the visualization. And, hey, it could happen. But the bottom line was Max was too busy. The guy who came up with *multitasking*, shit, that guy had The M.A.X. in mind.

So, anyway, Max was thinking that the Colombians were coming to town, and those dudes spoke, like, Spanish, right? So, you were going to be in bed with them, you better, like, speak their lingo. Seemed to make sense. And it was this kind of preparation that had made Max the *hombre* he was today.

Hombre. Man, he was getting this shit down fast.

He listened to the Spanish tapes whenever he got some downtime and when you were as freaking busy as Max, running a goddamn crack empire, there wasn't a whole load of free time floating around. He listened when he was eating, on the shitter; he even wore the fucking headphones in bed, letting that crap seep into his subconscious, so even his sleep gig was, like, working. Did The Donald know that little trick?

And sure, okay, it was a little uncomfortable—damn earpiece fell out and poked you in the eye and the wire got wrapped round your throat—but who said knowledge was easy. Fuck, you ever hear old Stephen Hawking complaining? And that dude was wired if anyone was.

Max laughed out loud, loving his wit.

A few times there, yeah, when he'd gotten a little carried away with the crack, the booze, he'd put on the tapes, let it crank, played that shit loud till Felicia had screamed, "The fuck is wrong with you, put on some Lil' Kim!"

The reason why she'd always be a follower, didn't grasp the big picture. The bee-atch just didn't get it.

One odd sidebar—the voice on the Spanish tapes had this, like, posh accent, like some Spanish royalty or shit, and Max could only speak the lingo in the same aristocratic tone. There was this Lopez dude doing the lessons and Max was incapable of speaking in a halfway decent Spanish accent if he didn't add "Señor Lopez" to everything he said, in that upper-class tone. Like if he wanted to say *"Puede ayudarme?"* in a normal tone he sounded like shit. But if he said, *"Puede ayudarme, Señor Lopez?"* he sounded like a native.

Man, he sure as shit hoped one of these Colombians was named Lopez.

Another problem, his vocabulary wasn't exactly massive. He wasn't going to be entering any Spanish Scrabble tournaments any time soon. And a lot of the phrases he knew weren't exactly useful. Like how many opportunities would he have to say, *"Usted tiene gusto de dos limones y de dos naranjas, Señor Lopez?"* Would you like two lemons and two oranges, Mr. Lopez? Or *"A que hora abre la oficina de correos, Señor Lopez?"* What time does the post office open, Mr. Lopez? Or, *"A donde esta un buon restaurant in este ciudad, Señor Lopez?"* Do you know where there is a good restaurant in this city, Mr. Lopez?

The Colombians might find it a tad odd that he was asking them what time the post office opened and where the good restaurants were since he was the one who lived in fucking New York. Or, make that *Nueva York*.

Eh, The M.A.X. would pull it off somehow. He always did.

He pushed the CD player away, went, *"Usted tiene gusto de más blow, Señor Lopez?"* and cut a fresh line.

Sha-Sha shifted on his water bed, couldn't get comfortable. When you weigh in at four hundred pounds and change, comfort, man, that shit's hard to come by.

He was twenty-six years old and where was his life at? Nowhere, that's where. He was doing the same old, same old all the time, every day, and he was getting tired of all that bullshit. He was still out there on the corners, busting his ass and for what? He wasn't The Man—shit, he wasn't even on his way to being The Man. Niggas sixteen and seventeen were above him, bossing his ass around and shit, goin', "Do this, Sha-Sha, do that, Sha-Sha, smoke that dude, Sha-Sha, how come you fucked up, Sha-Sha? Where's my money at, Sha-Sha?" Man, he was thinking about going out there one day, blowing all their asses away. He get a piece and a hundred bullets and solve all his damn problems.

But Sha-Sha knew why he was where he was at—cause he was a sick-ass, that's why. How many times he go to nigga above him and say, "I wanna move up," and the nigga go back to him, "Fuck you"? Sha-Sha knew it was his own damn fault, cause he had no damn self control. He didn't know how to stop hurting people and even the gangs, man, they didn't need no crazy-asses hangin' around. Like sometimes Sha-Sha would be walkin' down the street, and he didn't like the way some nigga was lookin' at him, or he didn't like his sneakers, or the way he smelled, or sometimes there was no reason at all, and he'd take out his nine, pop the motherfucker in the head.

Sha-Sha didn't know why he was so fucked-up—it was just the way he was. It was probably the reason why he got so fat. Whenever he got down about his life and shit, he'd go for the menus, order in a whole mess of food. Then he'd get on the scale, see he'd gained another ten, fifteen pounds, and he'd feel so bad about it, he'd go out and shoot somebody. Then he'd feel bad about how fucked up all that shit was and he'd start with burgers and pizzas again. It was like his life was going round and round in circles and there was no way out.

When he saw he'd passed four hundred pounds he was all ready to say, Fuck it, and go out and start killing people, and kill himself while he was at it. Didn't make no damn difference anyway and, besides, how long before the cops got off their asses and busted him? They'd already had him in for questioning three times for killing three different motherfuckers. Yeah, he'd been away, but never on a murder rap, and his fat ass wasn't gonna be doing no thirty-to-life upstate. Them niggas loved big boys and he wasn't gonna be gettin' jammed like a pin cushion for no thirty years.

Then Felicia, his ho cousin, showed up at his crib. She was looking fine too, with that big ghetto ass, but what she'd do to her titties? Every time he saw her they got bigger and bigger; now it looked like they was ready to explode.

He went to hug her, was ready to push her head down so she could start sucking on his dick like when they was kids, but she pushed him away, started dissing him about his weight and shit. Man, he was ready to smoke that ho, then she hit him with some big i-dea. Shit didn't seem so bad neither—get some cash and product off some white people and dealers from down south and shit. Twenty grand was bullshit, but maybe they could get forty for the product. That made sixty grand and that wasn't too bad. It got Sha-Sha thinking, anyway—maybe he didn't have to go out, start killing people after all. Sixty grand, shit, he could use that— start up his own crew with his boy Troit. They could be the ones ordering all 'em niggas around and shit. Yeah, Sha-Sha saw his whole life changing. He'd go on the Slim Fast and Lean Cuisine, drop a couple hundred pounds, be able to get up out of his water bed without feeling all that shame and shit.

So when Felicia talking, Sha-Sha kept saying Yeah, yeah, let's do it, let's take the white man's money. Stupid ho thought she was gonna get twenty grand, meanwhile she wasn't gonna get a damn cent. Then he fucked her good and sent her ass back to Manhattan.

A few days later, she called him, told him she knew where the drug deal was at. But she was acting all smart and shit—said she wasn't gonna tell him nothing over the phone, that she had to be in the car with him and Troit and then she'd tell them where it was at. Yeah, she was smart all right. Soon she was gonna be dead too.

Felicia came back to Brooklyn the day before. In the elevator going down, Sha-Sha pulled stop and made Felicia blow him before they went to pick up Troit. Sha-Sha had hooked up with Troit up at Sing-Sing. Troit looked the opposite of Sha-Sha, bone thin, no meat on his whole body, but he was just as fucked up in the head. They called him Troit, cause he was from Dee-troit. Rumor had it he'd killed so many brothers over there he had to come to Brooklyn to cool down. Most times when niggas started going on about all the people they popped, Sha-Sha knew that was bullshit talking. But he'd seen Troit in action and the boy was stupid-crazy. Sometimes after Sha-Sha killed somebody he felt bad and started eating and shit. But Troit, man, he didn't give a shit.

So they was all three in a jacked BMW—Sha-Sha driving with Troit up front next to him, and Felicia in the back seat. She was all excited and shit, talking about the twenty grand she was never gonna get. She even had a damn suitcase, said she was gonna leave New York tonight, get on a bus to St. Louis and open a beauty salon or some stupid shit like that. She still wouldn't tell Sha-Sha where the deal was at—just kept on with the "Make a left here, make a right there" bullshit, like she was Miss Shadow Traffic. Man, Sha-Sha was sick of taking orders, specially from his ho-ass cousin.

They took the Belt Parkway, round to the BQE. Looked to Sha-Sha like they was heading to Queens someplace. Sha-Sha and Troit just wanted to listen to jazz, have some peace and quiet in the car, before they had to go start killing everybody. But Felicia kept going on and on, givin' more mouth. She was talking about Sha-Sha's body again, saying how he was too damn fat, and should go for one of them operations where he could get his stomach sewn up or cut off or some shit. Then she started getting into it with Troit, telling the man he was too thin, that he looked like a skeleton. Sha-Sha couldn't believe it. Didn't the ho know who she was talking to?

Troit couldn't take any more and turned round and said, "Bitch, you better learn how to shut up."

Felicia still couldn't keep her mouth shut, said, "You better stop callin' me bitch. I gotta listen to that shit all day long from Max, and I sure as hell ain't takin' that shit from y'all niggas."

Sha-Sha saw Troit's hand go for his piece, knew what was gonna happen next. And he couldn't let that shit happen—not till they knew where the drug deal was at anyway. Sha-Sha turned to Troit, gave him a look that said, *Later, man,* and Troit put the piece down.

Felicia didn't shut up the rest of the ride.

One point Troit said to Sha-Sha, "Later, yo, she mine."

Felicia, all bitchy, went, "What he say?"

Sha-Sha, smiling, went, "Nothin'."

Thirteen

*I would have killed more but I was out of ammunition
and I was afraid to buy more.*
FRANCIS BLOETH, WHO SHOT
THREE PEOPLE ON LONG ISLAND

To get cash for New York, Angela and Slide ran a series
of fast guerrilla hits. Went like this: Angela would go
into a bar, lure some sucker, checking out his wallet
first, and then bring him outside where Slide got up
close and personal. They did seven of these stunts in
two days, knowing the Guards would be on them fast.
Three paid real fine dividends and the others, well
fook it, they were a bust, what can you do?

Still, they had their stake and Angela booked Conti-
nental direct to New York.

They ditched the shack they lived in and the car,
well, you couldn't give the frigging thing away, so Slide
stripped the plates, left it at the airport.

He was like a kid, excited at his dream coming true.
Annoying the goddamn shite out of her with the end-
less questions: Can we go to a Yankees game? Can we
live in Tribeca? Can we buy a Chevrolet? Can we go to
Niagara Falls? Can we, can we, can we, till she roared,
"Can we give it a fucking rest?"

He bought a new suit. It was June and she told him
it was going to be hot, hotter than a motherfucker, so

he bought a linen job, and was pissed when it creased on the plane. And, yeah, he bought a fedora, in white, looking like a poor relation of Truman Capote, and new shades—the real deal, Ray-Ban aviators. When the flight attendant came by with the beverage cart he ordered a Tom Collins and when that wasn't available, he went Bogey, snapped, "Gimme bourbon, rocks, Bud chaser."

To hear this in an Irish accent is to have lived a little beyond yer sell-by date.

Angela had a large vodka, hold the mixer. She wanted that raw burn of alcohol in her gut and she got it all right.

The in-flight movie had Tom Cruise in it and Slide went, "I love the Cruiser. Maybe we should become Scientologists, there's serious wedge with those dudes."

Angela had some Xanax stashed in her purse and over dinner, with those mini bottles of wine, she knocked those babies back and it knocked her right out. The last thing she heard was Slide asking the stewardess, "You got a carton of, like, Luckies?"

She thought she might seriously hate him.

Entering Kennedy Airport, Slide's first response was, "Holy fook!"

Angela's response was slightly different. She felt relief, hearing the accents, seeing the American flag, like, everywhere, and knowing she was, if not home, at least on familiar terrain. New York was her town; she knew how it worked.

Slide's Irish accent had got him through Immigration

and he got the 90-day visa. Angela had her American passport and she got, "Welcome home."

Outside Kennedy, they had to join a line for a cab and Slide was marveling at everything, going, "Fook, the taxis are *yellow*."

He wanted to skip the line, said, "Let's jump the queue."

She explained two things, slowly and patiently because her head was, like, fookin opening from a migraine: "One, you want to get killed in New York, try skipping the line. And two, that's what we call it here, a *line*."

Nothing could dampen Slide's enthusiasm and he said, "Could do me a line of coke right about now."

Online, she'd found a hotel in the Village, got two weeks at a decent rate, the Euro finally working in her favor.

The driver, a surly black guy, said, "The flat rate is forty-five bucks, plus tolls."

Slide, into it, went, "Jaysus, I'm being mugged already."

Either the black guy didn't understand the accent or he could give a fuck.

When Slide saw the size of the hotel room, he said to the bellboy, "Okay, we've seen the closet, now where's the room?"

Angela shushed him said, "Give him five bucks," and then tried to explain to Slide about tipping.

He listened with astonishment, then said, "Scam city, what a con."

Angela said she needed a shower, a big drink, and a lot of sleep.

Slide said, "You grab some z's, babe. Me, I'm gonna paint the town red." Angela was going to have to talk to him about his awful idea of what constituted current American speak, but she was exhausted from the flight and decided the slang lesson could, like, wait.

Slide hit the street, figuring he'd off his first American after a cold one or two. He fully intended chasing the serial killer record and he was in the right city to start. As he entered a bar he hummed a few bars of *New York, New York*.

The place was quiet. A guy at the counter was alternating between sipping a Coors Light and a pint of water. He had on those grey-tinted shades that shouted, Serious intelligent dude. He was reading the sports page.

What the hell, Slide was in the mood to talk, so he grabbed the stool next to the guy and asked, "How you doing?"

The guy shut the paper with a sigh, turned round, gave Slide a serious intensive look, then asked, "Irish?"

Slide was a little put off, thought he'd got the New Yorker thing down, but said, "You got me, pal."

The guy flicked his hair and said, "I know an Irish guy and, well, what can I say? He sure can talk."

Slide wasn't sure if this guy was fooking with him so he shouted to the bar guy.

"Hey, before Tues, right?"

That's some New York speak for ya.

The guy took his sweet time getting his arse in gear but finally came over and said, "What do you need?"

Slide didn't like the guy's tone, thought maybe he'd off both of the fucks, get a jump start on his record. Then he said, "Gimme a Wild Turkey, beer back."

The guy next to Slide exchanged a look with the bartender and Slide thought, *You guys dissing me?* Then he asked the guy, "You want to join me in a brew?"

The guy said he'd have another water. The fook was wrong with him?

The drinks came and the bar guy asked, "You running a tab?"

Slide stared at him, wondering what the fook was he on about.

The guy beside him said, "He means would you like to pay now or pay when you're done? How it works, you put some bills on the counter, and he takes the money as you go along."

Without thinking, Slide went, "Touch my cash, he'll be touching his right hand, wondering where his fingers went."

The guy laughed, as if he thought Slide was joking.

Slide knocked back the Turkey, drained the beer, belched, and put his finger in the air, doing a little dance with it, signaling for more booze. He'd seen that in a movie and always wanted to do it. You tried it in Ireland, you'd be waiting a wet week for service but the Americans, they liked all that signal shite, ever see them play baseball, nothing but fookin signals, anything but actually hit the damn ball.

The second Turkey mellowed Slide a notch and he felt that familiar heat in his gut. He'd had enough of these guys and asked the bartender for directions to the nearest betting parlor. As a child, his old man used to take him to The Curragh, the racetrack in Kildare, and Slide could pick winners simply by looking at the horses in the parade ring. It was a weird and wonderful gift, but erratic, not always dependable. If Slide could have depended on that gift, he wouldn't have ever got into the kidnap biz.

Slide cabbed it to the Off-Track Betting tele-theater on Second Avenue and Fifty-third Street. It was five bucks to get in and he was going to argue but said, *ah fook*. Then, as he paid, the woman went to him, "You need a shirt with a collar."

Said it as an order, like this was the Plaza Hotel and he was, what, some low-life shitehead? He heard the voice, prodding him to lean over and strangle the old wench, but he thought, *Whoa, buddy. Easy now, partner*. There was probably CCTV everywhere around here and after the whole Keith Richards fuck-up he wanted to be a little more choosy about his next victim. The last thing he needed was the NYPD breathing down his arse.

He cocked his finger and thumb in the gun gesture, said, "I'll be seeing you in, like, jig time."

Around the corner on Third Avenue and down a couple blocks, he found a sporting goods shop. Bought a golf shirt with a collar and dashed back to the OTB.

He was already twenty-five in the hole and his stake was only a hundred to start. He needed to pick winners, and fast.

Unfortunately the horse-picking talent he'd had as a child in Ireland eluded him in Manhattan. In the race going off at Belmont, Slide loved the look of the seven. He bet half his stake on the horse, only to watch the jockey pull the rat up on the backstretch.

Quickly Slide's stake eroded. He was down to his last ten bucks. He was waiting by the TV for a glimpse of the next post parade, when he noticed a guy celebrating, high-fiving with other gamblers. The guy had long straight hair, a strong jaw—kind of looked like a poor man's Fabio.

Slide had heard the guy cheering home the winner of the last the race, the race where the pig Slide had bet finished dead last.

Slide went up to the guy and said, "Had the winner, huh?"

"You kidding?" the guy said. "I hit the Pick Six for the first time in my life. Can you believe it?"

Slide, real happy for him—yeah, right—went, "So how much that get yeh?"

"A lot," the guy said, smiling widely. Was Slide imagining it or was the smug bastard trying to rub it in?

"What's a lot?" Slide asked.

"Eh, about five thousand bucks," the guy said, still with that self-satisfied tone, like one lucky ticket had transformed him from lifelong loser to king handicapper. "For me that's not a big deal. I've been hitting winners left and right for weeks. Who'd you play?"

"The seven."

"The seven!" The guy said it so loud, people were looking over. "You played that piece of shit? That was the first horse I crossed out in my *Form*. I can't believe you played the seven."

Slide, gritting his teeth, went, "So you some kind of expert on American racing or something?"

The sarcasm couldn't have been more obvious, but the guy missed it.

"Yeah, you could say that," the guy said. "I mean, they say only five percent of all gamblers come out on top, and I guess since I'm in that five percent that makes me an expert."

A few minutes later, Slide watched the guy collect his winnings. He was such a high roller now that, of course, he tipped the teller twenty dollars, went to her, "Thanks, hon," like he was De Niro in *Goodfellas*. Then he bought a round of drinks for his gambler friends. Offered to buy Slide one too, but Slide declined, going, "I don't drink." He was on a sarcastic roll all right.

Slide stopped betting. What was the point? He had a more surefire way to make his stake.

The smug guy hung around for the evening harness racing programs. He won a few more races, bragging to the teller, "I'm so hot, you're gonna have to hose me down."

When the guy finally left, Slide tailed him around the corner. It was getting late—there weren't many people around. Near a construction site, Slide grabbed the fook by the shirt, pulled him beside a Dumpster.

And get this, the guy goes, "Hey, come on, easy on

the shirt, man, you know how much that cost me at Banana Republic?"

Slide needed to get the guy to focus so he broke his nose for openers. The guy, hurting and seriously pissed off, whined, "Whoa, come on, I have to do a big photo shoot tomorrow for *Crime Spree!*"

"Crime spree this," Slide said, then he shut the fook up with a few rapid punches, blackened both his eyes. Slide went, "Nothing personal," and then he kneed him in the balls and took his wallet. His heart sung at the sheer weight of the cash. Meanwhile, the guy was groaning, "Help me, help me," but it sounded like, *Halle, Halle.*

Slide bent low, face in the guy's face, and, almost lovingly, moved the guy's long hair from his ruined features.

It seemed to finally dawn on the ejit that he was in, like, deep shite and he croaked, "Are you going to kill me?"

Slide went, "Naw, I'm going to let it slide."

He paused for a second. Then he reached out and crushed the fucker's windpipe.

The guy had a very flash watch, looked like one of those high tech jobs. Slide helped himself to that, then gave him a kick in the head for luck. He laughed, said, "Lights out." Then he sauntered off, going, "No hard feelings, all right, buddy?"

Fourteen

All I have in this world is my balls and my word,
and I don't break 'em for no one.
AL PACINO AS TONY MONTANA, *Scarface*

This was going to be the day of The M.A.X., the big enchilada, the coming out party, the date that Max showed Señor Lopez who was *el jefe*.

The meeting with the Colombians wasn't till nine PM, but Max had been awake since five in the morning, running the details in his mind, a nagging worry about *Los Colombanos* refused to go away. The stress was really starting to get to him so he decided, Fuck it, and had a little pick-me-up, nothing too heavy, just a few tokes on the crack pipe to go with his caffeine fix. And he was thinking, *I should eat, get something in my stomach*, but he couldn't, so, what the hell, he had another tiny hit.

But the dilemma kept weighing on him—what the hell was he gonna wear? What were folk wearing to dope deals these days anyway? Did you go all biz, the suit, the power tie, handmade shoes? Or dress lethal, like you were casual but, hey, watch your mouth, buddy, cause I might look like Bloomies but I'm carrying, like, major heat so tread real fucking careful, you stupid Lopez fuck.

Yeah, that could work, he liked that touch of swagger, he was preening in front of his full-length mirror. Had his eyes developed that Clint Eastwood hardass glint? He tried narrowing his eyes but he couldn't see for shit when he did that.

Whoa-kay, chill baby, chill way on down and he would but his goddamn heart was like pumping a mile a second. He needed to look chill, so he put on a Yankees shirt, it was black, had the logo only on the collar, showed he was a sports guy but not, you know, showy with it. Then he put on Tommy Hilfiger black slacks, looking good, all in black, looking…what was that fucking word the French had…*nora*?…no, *noir*. Yeah, he looked noir as fuck.

Then the piece de resistance—the Glock he'd found in Kyle's suitcase. Sure he'd gone through the kid's stuff—you had to know who you were employing—and underneath the copies of *Hustler*, *Playboy*, and *Bust* he'd found it, loaded, with a spare clip. The kid had an automatic in there too, so he'd left that. The kid was too much in awe of him to ask if he'd taken it—one of the perks of being the boss, the help didn't get to quiz you.

He pointed the Glock at the mirror and couldn't get over how fucking *cool* he was. He let out his breath— shit, he could have made it in the movies—said, "Name it, mister," and heard, "Who are you talking to?"

For a horrendous moment he thought his reflection had spoken to him—Jesus, he'd have to ease up on the marching powder—then realized Kyle was behind him. How long had he been standing there and what was with that look, the kid's eyes stuck on the gun?

Max went for aggression—you're in a bind, go ballistic—and said, "The fuck you doing, sneaking up on a person, get your fool self killed that way, son?" He liked the almost black intonation he'd achieved there and the *son*, well, that was pure raw talent. Then he noticed Felicia was gone—he hadn't seen her in at least a couple of hours—and said, "Where the fuck is my bee-atch?"

"She said somethin' about havin' to do some shoppin' or somethin'," Kyle said.

Max noticed he had his bible with him and said, "You're not gonna be reading that around the Colombians, are you?"

"What's wrong with the Bible?"

"Do whatever you want," Max said, "but I think it's a big mistake. Religion—shows you're weak, you're living in fear of *Dios*. We want to show these *hombres* we're fearless, then they'll be afraid of us, get it?"

"I need Jesus by my side," Kyle said.

The dope was definitely cruising in Max's system and he had a ferocious impulse to cap Kyle, just for the hell of it. Max had been at the center of a whole blitzkrieg of murders but, like, get this, he'd never— what was the term? Oh, yeah, *smoked a motherfuckah*. Nope, but he sure as hell had thought about it a lot. It was Peckinpah type stuff—a lingering slow-motion shot of Max, cool as the breeze, drawing on a thin cheroot, and then spittin' some baccy from the side of his mouth. He'd been so loaded one night, he even went and bought some chewing tobacco—that shit was harder to get in New York than heroin. Then back at his apartment, the whole scenario opening up, he'd popped the shit in his mouth and, oh sweet Jesus, the fuck was with that taste? It congealed in his teeth, nearly removing one of his very expensive crowns, and then it nearly choked him. He'd cap some dude *sans* the chewing tobacco, maybe get some Juicy Fruit, leave a lingering freshness too.

He barked at Kyle, "The only good book you need is right here," and then he tapped his heart, thinking, *Fuck, how deep am I?* Maybe he'd go for a doctorate in metaphysics when this gig was wrapped—hell, he already had Buddhism down.

Kyle, the dumb cracker, as usual looked lost, said, "I'm lost."

Max sighed, decent help was, like, freaking impossible to find, he tried to put some fatherly patience in his tone, and like Pa Walton on crystal meth, said, "Son, what you read in your heart is the only line you ever need to remember." Max had lost his train of thought halfway through the sentence and in frustration, said, "We're gonna be dealing with some heavy dudes here, son. They see that book, they're gonna think you got a concealed gun in there."

Kyle said, "The Lord is my weapon."

Max, sick of the whole conversation, went, "The Lord better be packing, then."

Kyle stuck his hand out and Max, puzzled, asked, "You want to shake my hand?"

Sly little redneck grin from ol' Kyle who said, "I'd

like my Glock. That piece cost me a whole bunch of bucks."

Max, flying off into another one of his accents, said, "Don't you be giving me none of yer lip, boy, hear? You ain't too tall to take a whupping."

The *whupping* set off a drug hard-on and if Felicia had been there, he'd have given her a real whupping right now. "Now git yer ass in gear, boy, we is set to rock 'n' roll, you hear what I'm saying? You down, bro, you ready to chill with The M.A.X., you ready to ice these spics?"

He liked this rap so much he was sorely tempted to write it down, use it in his HBO series.

Kyle, an edge in his voice said, "Don't call them spics."

Max said, "Long as they don't call my play, *hombre*." He started hunting around for the shit he needed to make a martini. There was enough time, as long as while he was making it Kyle went and got the car. Like, right now.

Kyle stared at Max as he found a pitcher but fuck, no olives. Who the fuck was supposed to be doing, like, the housekeeping?

Oliveless, he turned to Kyle, and in his most sarcastic tone went, "Hello, the car, the ve-hi-cle...like, duh?"

Kyle had the vacant-eye look back and Max reckoned, no two ways about it, down there they were definitely giving one to family members or sheep. Hell, maybe down there the sheep *were* family members.

He said, "Our means of transportation, son. Or are

you thinking we should call a cab, say, Take us to our drug deal, Mohammed?"

He had to get these lines down on paper. Maybe write 'em up as a book one of these days, like those Hard Case books with those women on the covers. Max had never picked one up but, man, those guys knew how to use a pair of tits to sell a book.

Kyle said, "Oh, right," and he was gone, with his bible.

Max downed the martini. Wasn't bad, maybe he could do a second, wash his mouth out, take the acrid dope taste out of his gums. Naw, better not. Say what you like about The M.A.X., he knew his limits—oh yeah, he knew when enough was enough.

He put the Glock down the waistband of his trousers, in the small of his back, and went, "Ouch." Jesus, it was cold. Did he have time to warm it up? Could you microwave a gun? And it pressed against his bum sacroiliac, shit. He took the piece out, got his black suede jacket. It had that expensive cut, you saw it, you whistled, it said taste *and* platinum card. Yeah, after today, it was platinum or bust baby.

The jacket had a large inside pocket and he put the gun in there. Was the bulge too big? Ah, fuck it, he was good to go.

He had a last sip of the martini, said, "Bring it on, *muchachos.*"

Max and Kyle headed out to Queens in a Ford SUV. Max wanted to go in a Porsche, show the *hombres* what a hip, happening guy he was, but he figured they'd be in a limo and he wanted to be above them, looking down. Yeah, you need that height advantage in any business transaction. How do you think The Donald did it? And how many millionaire midgets were there in the world?

He had Kyle do the driving. What, you think The M.A.X. had time for trivial shit? Get real, buddy.

Crossing the Fifty-ninth Street Bridge, Max did a line on the dashboard, just to stay nice and juiced.

Kyle said, "Um, you think you should be doing that?"

Max inhaled, felt the rush, went, "Doing what?"

"That coke in the car, out there in the open an' all... you know what I mean?"

Man, that slow, muttering cornpoke drawl could start to get on a person's fucking nerves. Max caressed the Glock, thinking maybe he'd shoot Kyle in the foot, see how he liked that. For fucking Christ's sake, the kid was, what, becoming moral now? Thought he had a bible so that made him what, God? Max wanted to remind Kyle that he was the one who'd turned him on to this shit—the kid looked innocent but he was a god-damn enabler. But he didn't want to get into it now, when he was so focused, so *in the zone*.

About ten minutes later, they approached the meeting spot—the lot behind the abandoned ware-house, right along the East River.

Max didn't see any other cars in the lot. He wondered what the fuck was going on, said, "What the fuck's going on? Weren't the *hombres* supposed to be here before us?"

"There they are," Kyle said.

"Where?" Max said impatiently. He didn't see shit and was that line wearing off already? Goddamn bullshit coke. What happened to the Real Thing?

"Right over there," Kyle said.

Now Max saw two kids, teenagers, approaching the car, squinting at the headlights. One of the kids was wearing a Madonna concert T.

"Who the fuck are they?" Max said.

"The big one's Xavier and the shorter one's Carlos," Kyle said. "They're the Colombians."

Max would've thought Kyle was joking if the kid wasn't dumber than Forrest Gump. These were the cartel, the Noriegas of the zeitgeist? And, yeah, as soon as he found out exactly what zeitgeist meant, he'd use it more often. Meanwhile, he was seriously agitated.

"What kind of bullshit is this?" Max said.

There was no limo in sight; how'd they get here, on their fucking bicycles? They had goddamn piercings. And how old were they, sixteen?

"Hey, bro," Xavier said, still squinting badly. "How 'bout cutting the lights? You blindin' my ass."

The fuck sounded like he was from the goddamn Bronx—how much American TV did they get down in South America? He didn't even have a Spanish accent. Max had been wasting his time with all that Señor Lopez shit for this?

Kyle turned off the headlights and Xavier and Carlos came up to the SUV's driver-side window. The three of them started talking, laughing it up, like they were in a fucking high school parking lot. Fuck, maybe they could all go out for pizza.

Max, needing a pick-me-up big time, was getting set to do another line, about to snort it through a rolled-up hundred, when another car pulled into the lot, headlights blazing.

"The fuck is this?" Max asked.

"Darned if I know," Kyle said.

There was something about Kyle's tone. He sounded very un-Kyle—a little too quick, too prepared. It crossed Max's mind, *Was this some kind of set-up?*

Max felt a drip of white cold sweat roll down his back and he knew that was gonna fuck up the line of the shirt. He was thinking, Uh-oh, good this is not.

Two black guys got out of the car. One was skinny, one was huge, looked like Fat Albert. They were both in oversized basketball jerseys and were wearing backwards baseball caps.

Max went, "What the fuck is this? A goddamn nightclub?"

Then Max spotted the automatic weapons the guys were holding. He was too shocked to react. He just sat there, looking as dumb as Kyle, as the two black fuckers started running toward the SUV, firing. Glass was shattering, Xavier's head exploded. The top of it just like took off, went through the air like some weird Frisbee and Max was thinking, *Oh, holy fuck.*

Covered in blood, Max shouted, "Drive, you asshole! Drive!"

A bullet went into Carlos's neck, made almost a whistling sound—whoosh, and kept right on going, to

Colombia maybe. Then Carlos crumpled like a sex doll Max had once had and crushed in his excitement. More glass shattered, and finally Kyle turned on the ignition and the SUV started.

Ducking, Max shouted, "Go!" and Kyle sped away.

Max didn't know if he'd been hit. He didn't feel any pain but maybe his terror had blocked it out.

Bullets continued to spray against the car and then Max remembered he had the Glock. This was it, his *Scarface* moment, a chance to put everything he'd learned to work. He could be Tony Montana, he could kill a couple of *putas*. Seeing himself in one of the drive-by scenes in *Boyz n the Hood*, Max sat up and started unloading the Glock, firing wildly at first, but then he hit one of the guys—the skinny one—right in the chest.

Bullseye, got the bastard dead on. Man, Max could shoot—he'd brought down his first *hombre* and it felt fucking wild, it felt *right*. He should have done this years ago, what a goddamned rush. He couldn't resist screaming, "Hee haw! *Caramba!*" as the SUV sped through the lot.

Then Max looked at the parked car back there near the gate, caught a glimpse of the back seat. He couldn't believe what he was seeing. Was that fucking Felicia?

He wanted to blow the backstabbing little bee-atch away, but he was too stunned to shoot. Right there, the cunt who'd sold him out, in his line of fire, and he got trigger shy. Fuck, fuck, fuck.

Fifteen

When they drove into the lot, Felicia saw the SUV and the two Spanish dudes talking to Kyle at the window and she said to Sha-Sha and Troit, "Do me a favor, yo—don't kill the white boy, Kyle. He ain't done nothin' wrong and he was the one hooked us up to begin with, know what I'm sayin'? Maybe shoot him in the leg if you gotta, or some shit like that, but don't kill the boy, a'ight?"

She was hoping to hell they wouldn't turn, give her that dead-eye, I-fuckin-hate-you-bitch look they been practicing. Hell, with Troit, there was no practice necessary. Few dudes chilled her ass but, man, this motherfucker was born crazy.

Up front, they were chilling with jazz, goddamn Wynton Marsalis, and Felicia didn't think they was hearing a damn word she was saying. Felicia didn't like all this getting in with Troit bullshit. She didn't know why Sha-Sha had to bring that sick-ass along in the first place, why he couldn't keep it in the family and shit.

Sha-Sha braked the car and cut the tunes and said to Troit, "Hold up," and Troit went, "Fuck that shit."

Troit had his piece out and Sha-Sha had to take his out too. Damn, was they AK 47s?

Felicia said to Troit, "See? I knew you was gonna fuck all this shit up."

But Troit was already out the car and Sha-Sha was with him. Before Felicia knew it, they was both shootin' like they was in Iraq and shit, blowing people's heads off, blood going everywhere. Felicia heard Max screaming and she hoped he was gonna get it next. Yeah, she hoped that muthafucka suffered real bad 'fore he went straight to hell. Shit, she couldn't wait for that ol' crackhead to be dead, and it looked like Kyle was gonna be dead too. Shame, dick like that gotta go to waste, but what you gonna do?

The two Colombians went down—that was good— but then the S.U.V. started moving and, shit, was that Max stickin' his head out the window, screaming his ass off, shooting a piece? That flabby white no good motherfucker was *shooting*? He missed Sha-Sha, but he got skinny-ass Troit down. She couldn't believe it— bad-ass Troit taken down by the most useless piece of white trash she ever had in her mouth.

The SUV went right by Felicia and Max was looking at her, aiming the piece right at her. Funny the shit people'll think about when they think they time's up. She hadn't thought about her momma in years, didn't even send Christmas cards to the old ho bitch no more, but now she thinking, *Momma you save me now, I'm gonna come visit y'all, send some bucks too. Y'all see, I be a good daughter now.*

Max's eyes got all wide and shit, like he was gonna

start coming in his pants, but he didn't shoot her. Then the SUV sped away, out of the lot, and Felicia said out loud, "Fuck you, Momma! You never did no bullshit for me anyway! I don't care if I see yo' big, fat, ugly ho ass ever again!"

The money was gone but at least they got the rock. Once they split the profits up, she was gonna be on her way to St. Louis. She was nearly laughing now, so happy to be alive, and she yelled, "I'm goin' to St. Louis. Hell, yeah, baby! Hell yeah!"

Felicia watched Sha-Sha get the rock out of one of the Colombians' pockets. He stared at the guy for a minute, then put two more rounds in the guy's face, turned then as if something occurred to him, and kicked the guy in the head, twice, keep the numbers level, then came back toward her. The fat man didn't look too happy. She didn't know, but Troit, the psycho motherfucker, was Sha-Sha's boy, his back-up bro and shit. And, yeah, Sha-Sha's face showed it. He couldn't believe his boy was down.

Looking down at Troit's shot-up body, Sha-Sha was thinking, *Damn, man, why you gotta be so stupid and start shooting the motherfuckas so fast ?* If they got up close first, they could've ambushed the niggas, got the white dudes and the Colombians at the same time, and when everybody was good and dead they've could've got the rock and the money both. But cause Troit was so wild and shit, they only got the Colombians, and got his own ass killed too.

His head still buzzing from all the guns and shit,

Sha-Sha couldn't believe it. The nigga was *gone*, wasn't gonna come back ever. Man, why was the world like that? Why'd bad shit always happen to good people?

Sha-Sha looked up at the sky and wailed to God, "Fuck you! Fuck you, you sick-ass motherfuckin' piece of shit asshole prick-face motherfucker!"

He went back to the BMW, thinking, *This shit, this shit ain't right, some messed up shit goin' on with this deal*. But he had to get them the fuck outa there fast, cause he could already hear the cop cars coming.

Sha-Sha drove away and Felicia wouldn't shut her ho ass up. She kept going on, bitching about Troit and asking when she was gonna get her part of the money. Sha-Sha told her to shut her ass up, but she kept going on, giving Sha-Sha a damn headache. He was still seeing his boy, running towards the SUV, like the fool thought he be bulletproof. He could almost hear the sick-ass brother's voice, yelling as he ran.

On the Belt Parkway, going past the Verrazano, Felicia was still going on, "I want the money tonight. Let's go see whoever you gotta see right now. And don't give me no bullshit about it neither. You ain't playin' me for no sucker. And if you think I'm gettin' down on my knees again, suckin' yo dick one more time, you crazy."

Sha-Sha couldn't hear Troit no more cause the damn ho was screaming, drowning out his boy's voice. He felt all that acidy shit coming up, spat on his own lap, turned around, and shot a big-ass hole in the middle of the bitch's head.

"That'll shut yo ass up good," he said.

He felt better already. Yeah, he could do with a cold one, a little tote of some crystal, count his profit.

He got off the Belt, drove into some dunes and shit. Left the ho's body there for the seagulls to come eat. He reached down, took her bag, cheap damn Gucci reject shit, like her whole cheap damn reject life. Yeah, he'd heard her back there, hollering for her momma. He'd fucked her momma when he was fourteen and now he'd fucked the whole damn family.

He looked up at the sky, waved his big arms, shouted to the birds, "Dinner time, y'all! Got y'all guys some real fine dark meat!" Then he laughed hard, muttered, "Hope you fuckers like silicone."

Sixteen

*There are no saints in this world, only liars, lunatics
and journalists.*
IAN BRADY, *Moors Murderer*

Joe Miscali was hot to trot, literally. He'd had to go to
the can like four times already, had stopped off at
Duane Reade, loaded up on Imodium Plus, and had
downed like a half a box of the suckers. Now his guts
felt like they were knotted together with superglue.
This was it, his day of glory, bringing down Fisher, and
for pure bonus, a Colombian cartel.

It had been an uphill battle convincing his superiors
that this was the real deal, but his sheer insistence and
the opportunity to grab major drug dealers had proved
irresistible to the brass. With all the scandals recently
involving crooked cops, they needed some solid press.
Joe had even called the *Daily News*, got a crime beat
reporter named Ward to accompany the team. The
SWAT guys were pissed, their commander going,
"Fucking civilians, they screw up everything, and press,
are you outa your fucking mind?"

The commander was a serious hardass, suited up like
Armageddon was imminent, with enough hardware to
take down a small army. His team was all much the
same—macho fucks who gave him the hard-eye. They
chewed gum, racked their weapons and muttered among

themselves. Joe had a flask of coffee, not a great idea with the trots, but what the hell. Without caffeine, he'd be like a hooker without the fuck-me heels.

He'd offered the flask around and they gave him looks of sheer disdain, the commander going, "We don't need stimulants to do our duty."

The parking lot in Staten Island was open, exposed, and they'd arrived at the meet two hours early, quietly getting civilians out of the way. Cops were positioned on all perimeters—no way the dopers were going to break out of this ring of solid steel.

Joe, seeing the expressions of the SWAT guys, had said, "I want Fisher alive."

The commander, rolling the gum along his inside jaw, said, "They give it up, no prob...otherwise..." He let the threat trail off.

Joe was going to have to watch this asshole real close, or else the guy would waste everybody, and with the *Daily News* there, Joe was getting a real bad feeling. He was trying not to look at his watch, but he couldn't resist and the commander caught him and said, "They're late."

Ward, the journalist, had been talking quietly with his camera guy and now turned to Joe and said, "Be a major public relations fuck-fest if your guys don't show."

Joe felt his bowels burn and wondered if he should risk more Imodium. How many had he taken already?

The humidity was building and Joe felt a dribble of sweat roll down his forehead, sting his eyes. Then realized the press guy was staring at him, a smirk in place, and Joe snapped, "What?"

The guy shifted his position so he was right in Joe's face, said, "How's it work for you?"

The fuck was his problem? Joe asked, "The fuck's your problem?"

This seemed to really ignite the guy and he said, "You being Mr. Nice Cop, isn't that your rep? The one who gets results with, what, with *decency* and *understanding*."

Joe said, "Yeah, well, we don't all have to be hardasses. You do what works best."

The guy was highly amused. He gestured at the very empty parking lot, the non-happening parking lot, and said, "Gee, and I can see it's working out really well for you."

Joe tried not to rise to the bait, especially with the growing panic he was feeling.

He said, "I'm sorry you might not get your story."

The guy was smiling, delighted. "Oh, I'll get my story. A no-show is a great story. All this NYPD/SWAT action, all the taxpayers' money, in an election year, flushed right down the toilet. Hell, buddy, I couldn't ask for a better story."

Before Joe could respond, the earpiece the commander wore began squawking. The commander looked at Joe, then pulled the earpiece out and shouted to his team, "Stand down, abort! Stand down, abort!"

Joe, his guts in shreds, asked, "What?"

Like he didn't know.

The commander was standing, tearing open the Velcro strips on his vest. His eyes like ice, he said, "A drug deal went down tonight, major gunfire, and Fisher may have been involved. But, guess what *Detective*, it's not on Staten Island—it's out in Queens."

Joe, bewildered, said, "Maybe it's another deal… I mean…."

The commander pushed past him, hissed, "Yeah, right. Face it, you just took it in the ass, pal, bent right over for it."

The photographer was snapping off pics of Joe, the SWAT team, and the empty lot. Joe shouted, "Put that fucking thing down!"

Ward said, "No more Mr. Nice Guy, huh? Might lead with that. Whatcha think? Think it works?"

Five minutes tops and they were all out of there, except Joe. He was left standing in the middle of the lot, his hands shaking, his bowels in full revolt, his mind going, *She couldn't…could she?…Jesus, and I gave her, like, a hundred bucks…with another twenty to come…and paid for the meal, she could've, like, had anything on the menu…I didn't say go for the cheap special…I was nice to her, wasn't I?*

A homeless guy approached him, went, "Yo buddy, got anything for a man down on his luck?"

"Fuck you," Joe said, and then, part of his old good self fighting to re-emerge, he said, "Sorry, buddy," and gave him the rest of the Imodium.

Seventeen

Death makes a person hungry.
CHARLES WILLEFORD, *New Hope for the Dead*

Max was ravenous. He wanted junk food, Italian, Chinese, mountains of carbs, fizzy drinks, cold brews, a heap of coke. He wanted to go on shooting motherfuckers for hours, capping them good. He wanted, he wanted to kill the goddamn world, but first he was gonna have fucking Kyle's ass.

In the car, leaving the bloodbath, Max tried to figure out if Kyle had sold him out. He even put the Glock to the kid's head, threatened to play Russian Roulette, but the stupid hick still wouldn't spill. He just kept quoting from his bible—Ezekiel, Job, Jonah, fucking Ecclesiastes. Yeah, like any of that shit was gonna help him now.

They pulled over and Max tossed the Glock out the window, into the East River. Even under pressure, with the cops on his tail, riding the high of his first-ever murder, Max knew how to cover the bases. They dumped the bullet-riddled SUV on Queens Boulevard and hailed a livery cab into the city. He knew the cops would find the car, trace it back to him, but he had a story all planned.

In the cab, Max told Kyle exactly what to say when the police questioned them, but he wasn't sure if Kyle was listening to a damn word he was saying. Kyle was still praying, frantically turning pages of his bible, like he thought the faster he read it the deeper the shit would sink in. It occurred to Max, does Kyle even know how to read? Down where he was from didn't they all live in trailers and start working on their momma and poppa's farms when they were, like, thirteen?

When they got up to the apartment, Kyle locked himself in the bathroom, where he sat chanting more of that bible shit. Max, fueled on crack, was banging on the door, trying to get him to open up. Then he had an idea. Bible boy wouldn't like to be the cause of another man's suffering, now, would he? Max stormed into Katsu's room and—oh Jesus, the skinny little sushi chef was jerking off to a Jap porn movie.

Max went, "Fuck, you've been making my salmon maki with those hands!"

Then Max thought about all the sticky rice he'd been eating lately and wanted to yack.

Katsu stood up quickly, his boxers at his knees, covering himself and bowing, going, "Sorry, sir. Sorry, sir."

Max grabbed him by his hair and pulled him down the hallway to the kitchen. He grabbed the butcher knife, put it up to the terrified chef's neck, then dragged him to the bathroom and screamed to Kyle, "Okay, bible boy, get your grits-and-collard-greens ass outa that toilet right now, boy, or sushi man's made his last hand roll."

Katsu screamed, "Max crazy! Kyle, you listen to Max and open door right now! He not fucking round!"

Kyle opened the door a crack, saw what was going

on, and said to Max, "All right, all right! I'll come out, just let him be. Let him be."

Sounding like some John Lennon freak, like he was gonna go hold a fucking séance at Strawberry Fields.

"I want the truth out of you," Max said, "and if you tell me I can't handle the truth, trust me, you'll make my day, asshole."

He slit his eyes like Eastwood while going for the Nicholson hardass tone. He almost hoped Kyle wouldn't give in. It would be fun to cut Katsu, to see what it felt like to kill with a knife. He'd already shot somebody today; if he strangled Kyle afterward it would be like hitting the murder trifecta. Yeah, Max felt fucking omnipotent, all right. He used to think that word had to do with, you know, getting it hard, getting a woody, but now he knew what it meant, he fucking knew.

"Okay, okay. I told her," Kyle said, tears streaming down his cheeks. "We were in love, Mr. Fisher. I was gonna her take back down to Alabama and turn her into an honest woman."

"You sold me out? After all I've done for you?"

Max felt seriously betrayed. He was Tony Soprano, getting ready to whack Pussy. He was Pacino asking his brother if he'd ratted him out.

Kyle said, "I tried to stay strong, I tried to do Jesus proud, but I couldn't. I just couldn't resist her. That woman, she did something to me. I think…I think she might be Jezebel."

"Yeah, she did something to you all right," Max said. "She tried to get your ass killed, and my ass too. Who were the guys Felicia was with?"

"I…I don't know."

"Bullshit, she must've told you something."

Kyle waited then said, "She said it was her cousin, I think."

"Did she tell you a name?" Max asked.

Again Kyle wouldn't answer right away, slow annoying fuck, then he said, "Yeah…It was Sha-Sha."

Sha-Sha? What the fuck kind of a name was that? It sounded like a guy in one those new videos Madonna was putting out—her tight and old in purple leotards with black guys hopping around her.

Max smiled, said, "But you don't know anything, huh?"

"That's all I know, honest to God." He clasped his hands together, beseeching. "Oh, please, sweet Jesus, don't invoke your wrath, and may the lord god Abraham, the sons of the tabernacle grant you the true wisdom—"

With his free hand, Max gave him a slap in the mouth, said, "May you shut the fuck up?"

Then Max gave Kyle another wallop, and because it felt good to beat on somebody he whacked his chef on the head too, the fucking jerk-off.

Leaving the two assholes, he went into the lounge, flipped on the TV and fixed himself a tall, dry martini, never letting go of the knife. It was like an extension of him. Maybe he'd be called Max the Knife in the movie. Jeez, then there'd be a musical. Max couldn't wait to see it. Maybe they'd get Hugh Jackman to play him.

He cycled through the channels till he got to NY1.

And sure enough, the main story was the shootings in Queens. Fuck, talk about popping wood. They were talking about a lone gunman who took down some of the baddest mothers in these here United States. Well, not exactly but that's how it sounded.

Then someone handed something to the news lady, a sheet of blue paper. Breaking news, she said. An ex-stripper named Felicia Howard had been found, dead, off the Belt Parkway. *Bye-bye, bee-atch*, Max thought, then he heard a pair of loud sobs from behind him. He turned around to see Kyle and the freaking sushi chef, weeping in unison.

The fuck was Katsu crying for? Uh oh—Oprah light bulb moment—the little turd was giving the sticky rice to her as well? Christ, was there anyone in the apartment she hadn't been screwing? If they'd had a dog, would she have fucked him, too?

Max turned back to the news report. A cop named Miscali or something was taking the heat for some monumental screw up. At first Max couldn't follow it, but then he started to get the gist, in bits and pieces. Kyle and Felicia must've sold him out, but she'd given the cops the wrong location. But then who the fuck had shot Felicia? The only one left standing after the bloodbath had been Fat Albert—what was his name? Sha-Sha. But why would her own cousin shoot her?

Max's head was throbbing from trying to follow all the ins and outs of this, not helped by no food, but he was fucked if he'd ever eat another morsel that jack-off chef produced. Also, the sounds of Kyle's sobbing and wailing were seriously getting on his already frayed nerves. He shut the fucking TV off and stormed off to his bedroom, carrying the pitcher of martinis with him.

Max came to around ten the next morning. He was in his good smoking jacket, the one with M in gold on the pocket, and his stomach felt like a very large rodent was trying to gnaw its way out.

He wobbled toward the bathroom, then stopped, a thought hitting his very tender head, *The knife, where the hell was it?*

Nope, not on the floor. Then he thought, *Kyle*, and went to the living room, but the boy wasn't there. He did a quick tour of the rest of the apartment—no Kyle.

Well, screw him, he had to get to the bathroom, like, now. As he sat on the bowl, feeling as if his intestines were pouring out, he decided Kyle had run on home to Alabama. Maybe Sushi Man went with him, the good ol' boys down there, they'd sure appreciate cornholing some yellow meat, good for the skin. As another upheaval hit his tender stomach, he was sort of relieved he didn't have the knife—he might not have been able to resist the urge to slit his own throat, put himself out of his misery.

Then the doorbell rang. What the fuck? The doorman was supposed to screen visitors or God knew what vermin could just come up and ring his bell.

He staggered to his feet, gave his tender ass a wipe, and was about to answer the door when he thought, maybe it's Kyle. Eh, fuck him. Let the backstabbing bible boy sleep in the hallway.

Max started to walk away when a voice shouted, "Police, open up!"

Could Max have imagined it? Some side effect of the dope, the vodka…?

But the banging continued and a voice, said, "Police, open the fuckin' door!"

Max opened it slowly, then they pushed it open all the way. That cop from TV—man, this was some bad trip all right—forced Max onto the floor and cuffed him from behind.

"Party's over, big shot," the cop said. "Time to get your scummy ass downtown."

Eighteen

I want the legs.
MEGAN ABBOTT, "POLICY," IN *Damn Near Dead*
(2006, ED. DUANE SWIERCZYNSKI)

Angela was not a happy bunny. They'd moved from the hotel to a basement apartment on Sixth Street, right under a restaurant called Taste of India. When she'd dreamed of coming back to New York, this was not where she'd imagined being. Yeah, yeah, all New York apartments were small, but come on, you couldn't swing a frigging cat in this place, least not a live one. The ceiling was brown, either from nicotine, mildew, shite, or curry. She prayed it was curry. There was a constant pong of Eastern spice in the fetid air so the curry theory made some sense.

They had, count 'em, three rooms. You think, how bad is three? Well, one was a bathroom, then there was the so-called living room/kitchen—i.e., a hotplate and a kettle and barely enough room to walk—and the bedroom was the size of some closets, with one of those fold-up beds. Can you say cramped? And with Slide on top of her in every sense, she was on the verge of a scream every damn second. And worse, like they said at McDonald's, *he was lovin' it.*

They'd found the apartment, a sublet, on Craigslist. The rent was medieval, and that was before utilities. It didn't help the situation that Angela was beginning to have serious doubts about Slide.

The books he brought home—what was the deal with those creepo volumes anyway?

The Stranger Beside Me
Dahmer: An Intimate Portrait
Gacy, in his Own Words
The Green River Killer
Inside the Mind of Serial Killers

Not exactly light reading. And he didn't just read them, he fecking *studied* them, Told her he was going to write a screenplay someday. Yeah, like she believed that shite. Her last New York boyfriend, Dillon, had told her he was a poet and he'd turned out to be a ruthless killer, not to mention a right bastard. And Slide, the shifty fook, could hardly write his name. Besides, what was she supposed to do, support some writer and his hopeless art? She'd had enough of writers and their constant whining. She wanted a guy who'd hit paydirt.

Speaking of which, when she was doing laundry one day she'd found a wad of cash in Slide's jeans, hundreds of dollars. When she'd confronted him about it he'd said he'd gotten real lucky at the OTB. And that fancy watch—he couldn't even figure out how to use it, but would he part with it? Would he fuck. He said a guy gave it to him when he'd given him some action on his forecast for the playoffs. Yeah, like he knew baseball from hurling.

And the guns: He was collecting them, already he

had a Glock, a Colt, and, most worrying, what looked like a small bazooka. He said he'd got them at a stall in the East Village and they were only replicas—yeah, right. Angela knew all about fakes, just check out her tits.

But why would he want such firepower? Then, as she had her first margarita of the day—and sure, it was only a little after two in the afternoon, but a girl needed all the support she could get—she suddenly stood still, the frozen margarita frozen in her hand.

Al-Qaeda.

Jesus wept—he had the dark looks, had begun growing his beard, and was always wearing those shades. Then she gulped the drink, another horrific thought hitting her:

Airplanes.

How many times had he made her watch *Airplane!* on their little TV? God, one time, riding her, he'd even hollered, "We have clearance, Clarence."

And as she began to mix a fresh batch of the margs, she remembered the time he'd taken her from behind, and roared, "Incoming, ground control to Major Tom."

Sweet mother of God, and don't forget his attempts to blend in, to sound American. Didn't they, those sleeper agents, try to, like, assemble? No, that wasn't it, fook…assimilate. Didn't they try to do that? And above them, the Indian restaurant, that fucking stink that permeated everything—Slide never complained; he seemed to love it. Them terrorist types, weren't they like *hot* on spices and shite?

Angela looked at the pitcher of margaritas. Whoa,

hey, who'd been sipping from it? It was, like, way down. She'd had, tops, three, if even that, and it wasn't like she'd used that much tequila. In fact, if anything, she'd given herself a priest's ration—that is, mean and measured.

She sighed, thinking, What the fuck? It wasn't every day you discovered you were harboring a terrorist. Homeland Security would probably pay serious bucks to grab this sleeper agent.

As she tried to come up with a way to turn Slide in for cash, maybe become a national hero along the way, she saw, out of the corner of her eye, a large roach emerge from under the table. It was sauntering, like, with *attitude*. Frigging cocksucker, strolling across the puke-colored floor like he lived there. Well, yeah, he did, but not for much fucking longer.

She grabbed the mini bazooka, got it to her shoulder and said, "So, let's see if this baby is just a replica."

It wasn't. She blew a small hole in the wall and she missed the roach. The fookin thing scuttled away under the bed.

Her ears were ringing from the blast and she gasped, "It was fucking loaded." Then added, "I'm fucking loaded," and began to laugh—a high-pitched, hysterical giggling. The smell of cordite was overwhelming and she could hear pounding on the ceiling. What were the Indians going to do, spill some goddamn curry over this? They'd probably put curry on the roach too and call it lamb roachala.

She turned on the radio—Dixie Chicks coming in

loud and sassy. Then there was lots of banging on the door. Angela opened it and a small Indian woman, concern writ large on her expressive face, asked, "What happened?"

Angela said, "The hot plate, it, like, blew."

The woman was trying to peer inside, but Angela had blocked better and bigger folk than this. Then the woman pointed and said, "Your eyes."

Angela reached up and realized her eyebrows were gone. She covered, going, "But don't worry, the roach is okay," and closed the door.

She was high on tequila, adrenaline and sheer firepower. She thought, No wonder guys went ape over this stuff. Christ, it was better than coke.

She laid the bazooka down on the counter, went in search of the other weapons, and said, "Lock 'n' fucking load." But to her shattered hearing it sounded like, "Rock n roll"

Axl Rose would have understood.

Later, after she'd passed out and caught a few z's, Angela went to look for cigs. She'd been smoking Kools Menthol, what the Irish called the pillow-biter's cig of choice. There were crushed empties all over the floor, but she figured, let Slide clean up. Right. Fucking A.

She went to the tiny cupboard, and pulled out the drawer that Slide kept his undies in. She rooted around and hello, the fuck was this? Wads of notes, Franklins. Jesus, he'd been holding out on her, the dirty bastard. And, whoa, what was this? Some kind of list?

In his very distinctive script—walloped into him by the Christian Brothers, or so he claimed—it read:

> *THINGS TO DO*
> *Beat the serial record*
> *Load up on weapons*
> *Dump the bitch after*

She paused, wondering, Did he mean her? And after what? A terrorist attack? Fuck on a bike.

Further:

> *Learn American*
> *Hit the gym*
> *Get vitamins*
> *Get hooked up*
> *Don't let it slide*

That was it. She had no idea what the last two things meant, and vitamins? What was up with that?

She closed the drawer with his white Y-fronts—and white they were, the screwball soaked them in bleach like some Magdalen Martyr. Then she counted the bills, thinking, Holy shit, where did he get all this anyway, his pal Osama? Wasn't that guy, like, loaded?

The idea of turning Slide over to the Feds had vanished. She skimmed a few bills, figuring, what was he gonna do, call the cops? Her hair needed a cut and color and she had to get her nails done. Then maybe she'd hit the Village, buy some decent clothes. And if she could, she'd have something done about her legs. Oh yeah, and she'd get some frigging eyebrows since hers were, like, *blown*.

She pulled a chair in front of the hole in the wall. It didn't do much to cover it up and she shuddered, imagining what might crawl out of there next.

Nineteen

Ah, well, I suppose it had to come to this. Such is life…
NED KELLY, BEFORE THEY HUNG HIM

Max knew this drill—the windowless, hot-as-hell room, no water to drink, uncomfortable chair. Fuck, they even tried the good cop, bad cop routine. Did these losers think that textbook shit could crack The M.A.X.?

Detective Miscali came into the room again for, like, the fourth time. Max was still wondering what a guy who looked like an Irish cop from Central Casting was doing with an Italian last name.

Miscali sat across from Max, and they said at the same time, "Did you kill Xavier Rivera and Carlos Fuentes?" Then Max said alone, "How many times are you gonna ask me the same stupid questions?"

"Did you or didn't you?" Miscali asked.

"I told you who killed them," Max said.

"Tell me again."

"The thugs who ambushed my SUV when I pulled over to take a leak."

"Were you conducting a sale of crack cocaine with Rivera and Fuentes when the attack occurred?"

"Absolutely not."

"Were you alone?"

"No, I was with a friend of mine."

"What's the friend's name?"

"You seriously asking me this shit again?"

"Tell me his fucking name."

Max breathed deep, then said, "Kyle."

"Kyle what?"

"I don't know."

Max said this definitively because, unlike practically everything else he'd told Miscali, this was the truth.

"You don't know your friend's last name?" Miscali asked skeptically.

"That is correct," Max said.

"Now why is that?"

"Because I never asked him it."

"Yet he's a friend of yours?"

"Yes."

Miscali leaned back, rolled his eyes, said, "And tell me again, why were you going to Costco?"

"Because I like to shop in bulk," Max said. "Saves money. I might look like The Donald, but that doesn't mean I throw money away. I've got deep pockets but short arms, if you know what I'm saying."

Miscali gave Max a look that screamed, *Gimme a fuckin' break*. Max, looking as bored as possible, gave a theatrical sigh. He remembered that time before, when they'd hauled him in over his wife's murder and he'd been assigned some snot-nosed kid lawyer who didn't know shit from shinola. He wouldn't need some idiot lawyer this time.

"Come on," Miscali said. "You expect me to believe a savvy, successful, sophisticated businessman like you has to go bulk shopping?"

"You cops probably don't have to worry about the

grocery bills but a businessman like me, I have to keep an eye on the small stuff, can't pay top whack every time I need a loaf of rye."

He thought, Let them digest that, see who they were dealing with. The corruption slur, which he hadn't outright said, hung there and the Miscali guy—oh, he got the dig, all right—looked like he might come over the table at Max. Then the other cop, the heavyset black guy named Phillips, came into the room, sat. Before, Phillips had been the bad guy and Miscali had been the good guy. Max wondered if they were going to try the old switcheroo. Seemed that way because Phillips gave Miscali a look, like, *Lemme handle this*, then went to Max in a puppy-dog tone, "Mr. Fisher, you expect us to believe you were traveling in a vehicle with..." He checked his notebook, as if he'd forgotten already, "...this *Kyle*, and you don't even know the fella's last name? And yet you want us to believe he's a friend of yours?"

Max knew the routine, he'd watched his *Law and Order*, had the good cop, bad cop gig down cold. Because he knew it would piss their asses off to no end and he was sick of being so—what was the word?—appeasing, he said, "Detective, when you've been in business in this city as long as I have, you acquire a lot of friends; remembering their last names is a task, alas, that even I, sometimes, am not up to."

That was the way—they wanna use words, right back atcha, asshole. He let the black bastard know who he was, subtly, and let the hint of the juice he might have leak over the words.

Before Miscali could jump all over it, Max added, "I do remember the mayor's last name, by the way. You want me to give *him* a call?"

Max sat back thinking, *Suck on that, detectives.* He watched Miscali's face and the sheer rage there catapulted him into a realization. Man, this guy had such a hard-on, such a ferocity about him, it couldn't just be because of a busted drug deal. There had to be more there.

"Tell me about Felicia Howard," Miscali said.

"You know her last name," Max said. "Good work, detective."

Miscali looked look like he was going to lose it. "Who was she working with?"

Max exchanged menacing glares with Miscali for a few seconds, then the dots connected. Felicia had been snitching to this fuck and now she was meat; the guy was shredded but he had to bite down and not blurt it out. Knowledge was power and Max wasn't yet sure but knowing this, he thought he could get one over on the guy. He went with, "Don't I get a phone call? And a soda would be good now. You guys have any Fresca?"

Phillips—now it was Good Cop's turn—grinned and went, "Aw, c'mon now, Mr. Fisher. You're gonna lawyer up? We're trying to help you here."

Max had the upper hand now, felt the delicious thrill of it, drawled, "Like I said, a soda would be an enormous ol' help right about now, and a phone call, that would be, like my friend Kyle was fond of saying, a gift from the Lord."

Miscali lost it, stormed over the desk, grabbed Max, tearing his good shirt, a Van Heusen, for Chrissakes.

Max went, "Whoa, you know how much these suckers go for in Bloomies?" Thinking, *Two shirts down the shitter in twenty-four hours? For fuck's sake*.

Miscali snarled in Max's face: "You fucking prick. You know the mayor, like fuck you do. You keep this up, you're gonna know a bunch of guys at Rikers intimately, if you get my drift. These guys, they're itching to run a freight through some asshole. You that asshole, Fisher? Huh, wanna make some new friends?"

Max was going tell Miscali that he'd already had a Chinaman in Alabama visit his asshole—been there, done that—but he didn't see the need to dignify the cop's remarks.

"Face it," Max said. "You took your best shots at me and I blew 'em all to bits. Got anything else to throw at me or can I go home now?"

Miscali glared at Max for a few more seconds, then he and Phillips left the room. Max couldn't help feeling seriously proud of himself. Talk about courage under fire.

Then, about ten minutes later, Miscali returned, smiling widely, a big toothy grin.

"Jesus Christ," Max said, "what're you gonna do, be Mr. Good Cop now? How long is this fucking circus act gonna continue, because I have to, like, be places, you know what I mean?"

"I'd cancel my dinner reservations for tonight if I were you," Miscali said. "Maybe you should cancel them for the rest of your life. Well, that's not true, but you'll have no choice of where you eat. And that prison grub will probably be a little disappointing to a classy guy like you. You know what I mean?"

Max didn't know what he meant, went, "What do you mean?"

Still smiling, Miscali said, "We just got some good news. Well, good for us, not for you. We just picked up your friend Kyle at the Port Authority, trying to board a bus to Mobile. It's Kyle Jordan, by the way. Your friend's last name. Jordan. I guess we'll see how the Costco story and the other bullshit you handed us holds up, or doesn't hold up. Meanwhile, I'd suggest you make yourself nice and comfy, Mr. Fisher."

Max knew he was fucked but good. He'd finally hit the end of the line, his winning streak was over. Well, it made sense—after all, how long could all the good cards keep coming his way? He'd been on such a great run for so long, but even the biggest winners in the world eventually had their luck turn to shit.

He just couldn't imagine that Kyle, Retarded Kyle, would be able to keep his story straight. He'd probably get so freaked out about spending eternity in an eight-by-ten cell with a guy named Lucifer on the next bunk that he'd put Max at the scene, put him with the gun, even describe how Max had shot that gangbanger. Yeah, Max was fucked, all right.

The way he saw it, he had two choices: cry like a baby, or go down with class. The old Max would've picked door number one, no doubt about it. But the new and improved Max was beyond all that whiny bullshit.

Max sat in the corner of his cell, got into a lotus position. Okay, okay, so he was about as flexible as a dead tree, but he was almost able to sit Indian-style. He started with the breathing and relaxation, then he threw his mantra into the mix. He wanted to go inward, remove himself from the physical world, but he kept thinking about coke. He'd been okay during the interrogation, but now he was feeling it in a major way. Whenever he'd meditated lately he'd done a line or two, just to loosen up, and without it he felt lost, unstable. Then Max shuddered, thought, *Am I an addict?*

The idea seemed absurd. The M.A.X. a cokehead? He was too strong, too focused to actually become dependent on something. He was using the coke, the coke wasn't using him.

Or was it the other way around?

Now Max was losing his focus big-time—all he could think about was that bag of coke on the coffee table at home. Then he had a thought that terrified him: What if the cops got a warrant and searched his apartment? He'd left a lot of shit around—the coke, some crack here and there and, oh yeah, some pot—and there wouldn't be a shortage of drug paraphernalia. If the cops wanted to bust him they didn't need a confession or evidence he'd been involved in those shootings; all the evidence they needed was in a penthouse on Sixty-sixth and Second.

Max caught a vision of the immediate future—the booking, the circus with the media.

Then the jail time. He noticed the big buck in the next holding cell, one real big mean-looking dude who'd been eyeing The M.A.X. Oh yeah, wouldn't he like to give Ol' Max the railroad treatment. Fucking Miscali—if they'd wanted Max to fess up, all they'd have had to do was *suggest*, just *hint* they were gonna buddy Max up with that Afro-American boy, and he'd have confessed to the freaking Lindbergh kidnapping and thrown in the little beauty queen as well. What the hell was her name? Bon...Bon fuckin' something. Jesus, the powerhouse intellect was winding down, even The M.A.X. got tired. What was it he read somewhere? Homer nods? Like in *The Simpsons*? No shit, he was zoning, going in and out of thoughts, didn't realize he was muttering aloud till the homeboy next door growled, "Shudthefuckup."

Christ, Max tried but the words just came spilling out. This is what happened when you were hyper-aware, mega-bright, the flow couldn't be stopped. You could cage it but, man, you could not contain it.

Max began to weep. What had he done? Really now, come on, hadn't he just tried to get a slice of the American Dream? And tell the truth, was anyone hurt? Okay, yeah, the black guy he'd capped but, man, that was one fucking rush. He wished he had that Glock now—would blast the fucker in the next cell first, cap him right in the balls, then blast his damn way right out of this freaking hellhole.

Was the little girl's name Bon Jovi?

About an hour later a guard approached the cell. Max looked at the guard, anticipating the barked command of, "Get your ass in gear, dickhead."

What he didn't expect the guard to say was, "You're free to go, Mr. Fisher."

Twenty

I like to beat up a guy every now and then. It keeps me hand in.
MONK EASTMAN, NEW YORK CRIME BOSS

When Slide got back to the apartment, some Indian woman grabbed him and started screeching about an explosion in the basement and how she wouldn't tolerate this type of behavior. Slide was tired, wanted to get inside, get a cold one, many cold ones, and here was this mad Indian cow yelling in his face. He was sorely tempted to off her right there, but he sighed, said, "Yeah yeah, I'll take care of it."

She was still hollering, pointing her finger in his face, saying, "I will not stand for this" and "This cannot happen under my restaurant" and a lot of other shite talk. Finally he got away from her, went down to see what the bejaysus was happening in the apartment.

First thing he smelled was cordite. He was confused—had Angela been in a shootout? Then he saw the empty pitchers of margaritas and, worse, his list, his whole game plan, was out on the table. The bitch had been going through his stuff.

She was in the bathroom, the door locked. Slide busted open the door—wait till the Indian cow saw that—and grabbed Angela, pulled her out into the kitchen area. He whacked her good and was about to lay on a whole lot more when she shouted, "Get your fucking hands off me," and whipped out one of his handguns.

Stupid bitch couldn't tell the safety was still on? He grabbed the gun by the barrel, wrenched it this way and that while she fought to pull the trigger. Eventually he tore it from her hand.

Angela shrank back against the wall, went, "Oh, Jaysus, please don't kill me!"

Kill her? Slide wanted to ram her head into the wall a few hundred times, watch her bleed out. But he'd had a long, hard day—he'd killed a rollerblader in Riverside Park earlier—and he wasn't in the mood to kill again, not right now, anyway.

"You didn't call the police, did you?" he said, tossing the gun on the table.

"No," Angela said. "I swear on me mother's grave, no. Nor Homeland Security."

"Homeland Security?" he said.

Angela, trembling, went, "You're in…Al-Qaeda, aren't you?"

"Al-Qaeda?" Slide said. "Are you fookin' mad?"

" 'Cause what I've been through, with IRA guys…I can't take another terrorist boyfriend."

"Is that why you blew the place up? Cause you think I'm in with fookin' Osama? Jesus wept, are you stone mad?"

"Well, you're growing the beard…and you're always talking about airplanes and—"

Slide went to the fridge, opened a bottle of Bud, sucked it down in one sloppy gulp.

Then Angela, who'd regained some of her composure and her earlier anger with it, went, "In that case, Mister Not-Al-Qaeda, what's this list, then? You planning to dump me?"

Actually, especially after this, Slide was planning to do more than just dump her. But, because he loved to fuck with people's heads—it's what he lived for—he said, "Never, baby. We're a team for life."

Angela said, "Then why did you write those things?"

"It's for me screenplay," he said. "I have to have some way to get money for us, right?"

"A screenplay, my arse. Try again."

"All right," Slide said, smiling because a brainstorm had come to him just in time. "What can I say. You got me. I been havin' an affair—but I'd already decided to break it off." He picked up the list from the table, neatly tore it in two, put the pieces in his pocket. "It's her I'd decided to dump. Not you."

"You asshole," Angela said, but there was a hopeful glimmer in her eye.

"I love you, baby," Slide said. "You and me."

"You mean it?"

"Cross me heart."

"Who was she, Slide? Was she someone I know?"

"Who?" For a moment, he seemed completely baffled.

"The other woman, Slide. The one you're dumping."

Oh. "Nah," he said. "No one you know."

"Was she…younger than me?"

"Ah, fook, see why I didn't want to tell you? Enough with the questions already. T'would only hurt you to know."

She went over to him, wrapped her arms around him tightly, and said, "I just want things to work out for us so badly, and I don't want any more trouble. I was thinking—maybe we should leave New York."

"What do you mean? We just got here."

"Yeah, but I'm tired of living this way, in this fookin' coffin, with curry dripping from the ceiling. And I'm tired of the whole city grind. I want to move to the suburbs. I want to be a soccer mom. I want to have a big kitchen that I can cook in. I want to live in a big house in New Jersey, like the one the Sopranos have."

He had to admit, the idea appealed to him. Operate in the suburbs, be Mr. Low Key Guy, hold down a job during the day, kill at night—yep, that worked. And the Sopranos' house with that swimming pool! Angela, she could be like Mrs. Soprano. He could go around killing his arse off and she'd be there at the door at night to kiss him and say, *How was your day, hon?*

"I'd like that too, babe," he said. "But we need a stake to make that happen. I've been trying to get it, but it's just not coming together."

"Well, then," Angela said. "Take a look at this."

She showed him a photo in the newspaper, some business fuck looking smug.

"And that is of interest fookin how?"

Which was when she told him the whole long story, how she got mixed up with Max Fisher before she went to Ireland, had even been engaged to him for a while, and now he'd been connected to some drug dealers.

"You sure it's him?" Slide asked.

"I was engaged to the fooker," Angela said. "You think I can't recognize a snap of him in the paper?"

Slide said, "So he was arrested. What's that gonna do for us?"

"If you actually read the article you'd see that he was released, along with his partner, this guy, Kyle Jordan. God only knows how he got mixed up with that crowd. Max dealing crack—Jaysus, I can't even imagine that."

Slide went, "So what do you want to do? Kidnap him?"

"Not him—somebody close to him, and then make Max pay," Angela said. "See, I know how Max is. He talks the talk but deep down, when it counts, he's what we in America call a wuss. You should've seen him when he found out he had herpes. He was crying like a baby."

"Herpes?" Slide asked.

"Oh, no, he didn't catch it from me," Angela said quickly, obviously busted, trying to cover. "He got it from, um, a previous relationship. And he didn't give it to me either. Honest."

Slide suddenly felt the urge to scratch. He also had the urge to wallop her again, but the lure of money was stronger. He said, "So he's a wuss. What does that do for us?"

"He's in a very vulnerable position, cops breathing down his neck, and if he's dealing drugs these days, he must be seriously loaded. It's the perfect time to kidnap somebody close to him and the panicked bastard will pay."

"I like it," Slide said, "but who do we grab? He got a wife?"

Angela got a strange look on her face, said, "I sincerely doubt that any woman in her right mind would be with that man. But there's this partner—Kyle from Alabama."

"You know him?"

"Never heard of him before, and honestly I can't imagine what Max is doing with somebody from Alabama. I mean, the article says he met the guy down there. When I was with Max he bitched about going to the West Side."

Slide was playing with the idea, tossing it around in his mind. He wanted to get the kidnapping gig down and he knew it would pay serious wedge if only he could stop killing the victims so fast.

"The only problem," Angela said, "is how we do the abduction. After all, Manhattan isn't Backwoods, Ireland. You can't just nab somebody off the street."

"True enough," Slide said, grinning. "But *you* can."

Twenty-One

Denial is the outstanding characteristic of the addict.
ADDICTS ANONYMOUS

Max took twenty minutes to fill out the Cocaine Anonymous addiction test, twenty-three questions asking him things like whether his cocaine use was interfering with his work (*Nope. Moolah rolling in*), whether he'd experienced sinus problems or nosebleeds (*Occasionally*), and whether he felt obsessed with getting coke when he didn't have any (*Si, señor*). He tallied up the yeses—only eight out of twenty-three, nine if you counted the nosebleeds one. Hell, he wasn't an addict, not even close. What the fuck had he been stressing about? And, to think, he'd been seriously considering the idea of cleaning up, going into rehab. Whew, dodged a bullet there.

Max ripped up the addiction test and did three quick lines. Whoops, what was that blood coming out of his nostrils? Nine yeses. Eh, what the fuck ever.

The only downside of not being an addict was he couldn't do one of those rehab gigs. *People* magazine had done a piece saying you were, like, *nobody* unless you'd done at least one stint. That bony Brit chick Kate Moss—yeah, she'd fucked up big time by being photographed shoving mountains of coke up her dainty little nose. It looked like she was gonna lose all those lucrative contracts—so what'd she do? Yup, that's right, headed right to rehab in Arizona, and *voila*—not only did the dumb-ass public admire her for her courage but shit, get this, she scored more gazillion-dollar contracts. Now that was class. Them Brits, they had some sneaky moves—no wonder they'd once owned India.

So, Max thought, when he had his movie career up and humming, he might do a stretch in one of those places anyway, just for the PR bump. Not long—come on, how long could The M.A.X. be out of the game?— but yeah, some time to deal with "personal issues" would do him good. He could see the cover of *Entertainment Weekly*, The M.A.X. looking contrite and yes, suffering, in real, physical pain, but was he denying it? Fuck no, here he was fessing up, admitting—and this would make a killer headline—*I'm human, too*. A tear would be rolling down his cheek, of course, though they'd probably have to Photoshop that in. God, it would be beautiful and word was, in those clinics, you made the best dope connections so he could, you know, combine business and healing in the one package. And, chances were, he'd meet one of those babes like Paris Hilton, have her hanging on his recuperating arm. Nah, not Paris; he liked the way she'd talked into the mike in that sex video, but she was way too flat-chested and way too bitchy, a bad perfecta if there ever was one. He'd rather have that other one with the implants, Tara Reid? Yeah, that Tara babe would be all over him, oozing love for The M.A.X., and when the press asked he'd simply say coolly, "We're just good friends."

Yeah, he'd be all set if only the blood would just, like, freaking STOP. That stuff, it totally ruined your shirts. He was wearing a white Van Heusen number—it was fucking Goodwill for that baby. How many fucking shirts had he bled on and had to donate? A hundred bucks each for those shirts and they went right down the shitter. Maybe he'd have to start buying black ones, go the Johnny Cash route.

Max was totally gone on this whole vision when his thirst kicked in, an overwhelming, all-consuming passion for gallons of water. Ah, screw that, make it a brew, lots of vitamins in those hops and lots of yeast too, right? Yeah, just a cold one—hell, maybe a few cold ones—and didn't that prove he wasn't a coke-head? You never see a junkie gasping for a Bud, right?

"Kyle, The M.A.X. needs a brewski!"

Kyle was back at the apartment, but the sushi chef was gone. Maybe he ran back to Japan, or at least back to Nobu. Max had given Kyle Katsu's room but, man, Max hoped the kid had changed those sheets.

Max shouted for him again, then pounded down the hall to his room. The kid was watching Meg Ryan movies, a stack of 'em back to back—said he was having himself "a Megathon"—and he actually asked Max, "You think she'd be hard to find in Seattle?"

The schmuck really believed she lived there and, fucking with him, Max went, "I'll ask Hanks if you can have her address."

The kid's eyes got huge and he stuttered, "You know T-T-Tom Hanks?"

Times like this Max wondered—was he fucking with Kyle or was it the other way around? Could someone be alive and functioning and yet be so brain dead?

But Max said, "Me and the Hankster go way back. Yeah, he was unsure about doing this movie with a fucking mermaid, and I told him, go for it Tommy, it'll make a *splash*."

The kid was stunned and Max had to jar him out of it, going, "The brewski. You know before, like, Tuesday?"

Rooming with Kyle, having to dumb it down on a daily basis, was stretching Max's patience mighty thin, but it wasn't like he had a choice. The cops had released Kyle along with Max, with instructions that they couldn't leave town. Max didn't want Kyle living alone someplace where he could fuck up and do something stupid. Max figured he knew the cops' big game plan. They'd searched the apartment while Max and Kyle were being questioned but, guess what, they hadn't taken anything. They could've nailed The M.A.X., but for what? It was his first offense and they could get possession but could they have gotten intent to sell? Maybe, but maybe not. Maybe Max would've gotten six months or, if he had a good lawyer, community service. No, Miscali and those assholes didn't want to send Max up on bullshit charges. They wanted the Big Kahunas, the Colombian suppliers, the behind-the-scenes players. So they figured they'd leave Max and Kyle on the loose for a while—see where that led them. Little did they know that The M.A.X. was one step ahead of the game.

When Max had been released from the precinct, he'd spotted the tail on him right away. *Spotted the tail*—man, he had this shit down cold. He'd also seen cops around outside when he went out for chores—i.e., to buy cigars and load up on booze. The cops weren't uniforms and they weren't holding up NYPD signs, but they might as well have been. Max, especially when he was coked up, knew everything that was going on around him and he had amazing instincts. Put one cop in Yankee Stadium with fifty thousand screaming fans and Max would pick the cop out, no problem. It was like Max was born with sonar for this shit.

One afternoon, when Max left his apartment, he did his usual cop search, immediately spotting the son of a bitch—the black guy sitting at the table in the sidewalk café across the street and up the block. Then, as Max headed up the block, he spotted something else. Blonde hair, big knockers—could that possibly be…?

Max's hand was up, hailing a cab, and a cab pulled up, nearly running over his goddamn foot. When Max looked over again she was gone.

"Come on, buddy, get in my cab," the driver said. "I don't have all day."

Max got in, trying to look back to confirm, *Was it her?*

It couldn't've been, Max decided later. What the hell would she be doing in America, after all this time? Nah, it wasn't her—it had to have been a hallucination. Or maybe it was just paranoia. Okay, okay, so now he was up to 10 out of 23 on that coke addiction test. Maybe he shouldn't've ripped the thing up so quickly.

The hallucination, or whatever it had been, reminded Max of how lonely he was. Yeah, he had Kyle around, but Max was physically lonely. Since Felicia had been killed there had been a big gap in Max's life—well, two gaps, about the size of a pair of 44-double-E's. The thing was, Max was a relationship guy. Without a loving, caring, big-titted woman at his side he felt incomplete. Yeah he was a metropolitan dude, but at heart he was a romantic, a one-woman man. Sure he played around, but no biggie, that was just for show, to impress the troops. But deep down he was a Paul Newman type really—one woman, one love. Damn straight and, hey, maybe he'd invent a salad dressing too. Fuck, the possibilities were, like, endless.

Funny thing was, Max had been thinking about Angela for a couple of weeks now, wondering where she was, who she was with, if she was happy. Maybe that's why he'd thought he'd seen her, because she was prominent in his thoughts. So much had happened since the last time they'd spoken that it was hard for him even to remember what had gone wrong between them. He couldn't remember any fights they'd had or any real conflict. Okay, she'd given him herpes, but aside from that Max could only remember the good times—the blowjobs, the quickies on his desk at his old office. You know, the Hallmark moments.

The next morning Max couldn't get out of bed, depression kicking in big time. Even the thought of getting up for a little nose candy and some *Scarface* didn't have any appeal. Kyle, God bless the kid, noticed Max's state and tried to help, but The M.A.X. just couldn't be reached. Max was even thinking about retiring the The in The M.A.X. He just didn't feel worthy.

Man, this being depressed shit sucked big time.

Then, the next morning, Max noticed Kyle was gone. He thought maybe the kid had gone out shopping or to Blockbuster to get another Meg Ryan movie, but then it got to be afternoon and there was no sign of him. It was very unlike Kyle to disappear for even a couple of hours without leaving a note, or saying where he was going and when he'd be back. Sometimes Max felt like he was the stupid kid's father. And there was another virtue right there, his fathering side, his nurturing streak. No wonder people flocked to him—he had enough love to go around.

Max wondered if the cops had picked Kyle up and Kyle was busy confessing, implicating Max in the shootings, but the sad thing was that Max didn't really care. Having to spend the rest of his life as some queer's fuck hole seemed like a better option to Max than lying around in bed all day, feeling so, so...so worthless.

Sometime in the afternoon, the doorman called up, said there was a package for Max at the front desk marked URGENT AND PERSONAL. Max didn't have the energy to go down to get it so he had one of the porters bring it up. Max was so not himself that he gave the porter a five-buck tip. The porter, shocked, went, "You feeling okay today, Mr. Fisher?"

Max couldn't even muster the energy to fire back with one of his usual zingers. He just smiled meekly and muttered, "Have a good day."

The package was about shoebox size—actually, it seemed to be a shoebox. But there weren't shoes in it—it was way too light for that. An envelope was attached to the box and there was a note inside the envelope. Max took out the note. It read:

NOW WHO'S A DICK?

Even more confused, Max opened the package. It was wrapped up with lots of tape, and then inside there was crumpled-up newspaper. Max was starting to think it was some prank, maybe that cop Miscali playing head games with him, and then he got to the plastic bag, looked like one of those Ziplock things. There was something inside the bag, something long and pink.

Max held up the bag, studying the contents, and then it hit him. If he hadn't been so depressed he would've screamed—fuck, he probably would've run for his life—but in his current state his only reaction was to drop the bag on the floor and back away very slowly.

Twenty-Two

*There are few more lethal creatures than
an Irishwoman with a grudge.*
IRISH SAYING

Angela had been casing Max's apartment and, Jesus,
she'd nearly blown it. The other day he'd come out the
front entrance, right on to Second Avenue, and nearly
seen her. His face had taken on a stricken look, but
then a cab had pulled up and distracted him, giving
Angela a chance to duck out of sight.

She hated to admit it, but the bastard looked pretty
good. He'd lost weight and was wearing a classy suit—
shame about the beige, but it looked like Hugo Boss.
He still made her stomach turn, and yet he had a
certain air about him now, like he'd finally gotten it
together. She liked that he was clean-shaven as Slide's
bearded Arab look was starting to bring her down big
time, not to mention scare the living crap out of her.
She was impressed with how Max had hailed the cab—
no frantic arm waving, just a hand barely raised and
then the cabbie had screeched to a halt, knowing a
player when he saw one.

The next morning Angela was back in front of Max's
building when she saw Kyle, the young kid from the
newspaper article, coming out the front door. He
walked to the corner, waited for the light to change.

He had a forlorn country boy look about him, as if he'd hiked over here from the Ozarks or some place like that. He had a kind of cute face—in a lost, helpless sort of way. Best of all, as she walked up to him, swinging her hips slowly back and forth, she saw he was blushing. Every woman knows that when a guy starts blushing you're going to be adding notches to the bedpost.

Angela said, "Hey, handsome, anybody ever tell you you look like Brad Pitt?"

Angela had used lots of pick-up lines over the years but her "Pitt-Depp technique" had been her most effective by far. It went like this—if the guy had blond hair she told him he looked like Brad Pitt; if he had brown hair she told him he looked like Johnny Depp. Guys soaked that shit up every time.

Although Kyle looked nothing like Brad Pitt, she could tell the line worked big time as he blushed some more, then said, "Wow, thanks, ma'am. And you know who you look just like?"

"Lindsay Lohan," Angela said posing. She'd been to the hairdressers earlier and had asked for the Lindsay Lohan look.

"No, ma'am," Kyle said. "You look like Meg Ryan."

This was one Angela had never heard but, hey, maybe it was an Irish thing—seen one mick, seen 'em all.

She silently blessed that hairdresser, screw Lindsay Lohan, and she put her fingers to her lips and whispered, "Actually I'm Meg's half sister."

She'd meant it as a joke but he stammered, "N-no way."

"Way," Angela said, going along with it, thinking either this kid was putting her on or he was a total moron.

"Man, this is so awesome," the kid said. "I've seen all your sister's movies, like, a hundred times. Wait till The M.A.X. hears about this."

The M.A.X.? What the F?

"Have you seen *my* films?" Angela asked.

"You mean...you mean you're an actress too?"

"One of the best." Had this been Angela's easiest pick-up or what? She moved right in close, his blush getting a notch redder, then she said in what she knew was her huskiest tone, "How would you like a signed picture?"

She could see his boner hit instantly and, she had to admit, that excited the hell out of her.

She added, "I have a small apartment in the city, for when I'm planning a shoot. How would you like to accompany me there? You could help keep the press away."

He looked like he might pass out. Before he had a chance to even consider the sheer implausibility of any of this, she hailed a cab. Yes, she had to wave, a lot, but finally she got one to stop. She squished up close to Kyle, letting her breasts casually rub against his arm.

When the cab pulled up to the apartment on Sixth Street, the kid had zoned out, was in some kind of trance, and kept muttering stuff about Meg Ryan and Jesus. If they hadn't needed Kyle as ransom bait she would've dumped him somewhere because she was getting seriously weirded out.

She slipped her hand in her bag, took out a pair of shades and said, "So I won't be recognized."

She led him down to the apartment. Slide was stretched on the sofa and Angela went, "My agent."

Slide was impressed, asked, "How the fook did you pull it off?"

Angela turned to Kyle, whispered. "Why don't you wait for me in the bedroom and I'll sign the picture for you?" Then added, when he still hadn't moved, "And if you're a good boy, maybe I'll call Meg and let you chat with her on the phone."

Kyle hurried into the bedroom.

"The fook is Meg?" Slide asked.

"Meg Ryan." Angela posed. "You think we look alike?"

Slide gave her a once-over and said, "You're fookin' weird." Then he said, "Okay, better get to it." He went to the counter, picked out a knife with a six-inch blade.

"To what?" Angela feared she might have misjudged a boyfriend yet again. She lowered her voice to a whisper. "We agreed we'd hold him for ransom. You're not going to…hurt him, are you?"

"No, I'll be sure to give him lots of anesthesia," Slide muttered, smiling.

"Seriously, Slide." Angela was panicked. "Remember all the trouble you got into with that Boyo in Ireland. Don't hurt him."

"I'm not going to hurt him," Slide said. "I'm just going to frighten him, that's all, so Fisher can hear some begging and screaming when we make the ransom call. You want the money for the Sopranos house, don't you?"

This seemed logical, but somehow Angela didn't trust him completely.

She said, "Swear to me on the graves of your parents and your sister that you won't hurt him at all."

Slide had told Angela the sad story of how his family had been killed in a car accident when he was twelve years old.

"You know, I think you better leg it," Slide said. "You're ruining me concentration."

"Swear—"

"All right!" Slide exploded. Then more quietly, "I swear. Now would you go take a walk while I get him ready for the phone call?"

Angela turned and walked out, still wearing the dark shades. She headed up Sixth Street. She didn't know how she'd reached yet another new low in her life. For a while things had seemed so hopeful—she'd just wanted to have a happy life in the suburbs, a couple of kids, the swimming pool—and now that poor kid was in that apartment with her latest monster boyfriend, and it was because of her.

Fuck him, she decided. She'd do kidnapping with him, but she wasn't gonna do murder. That poor kid— he'd really thought she was Meg Ryan's sister, and maybe that he was gonna get laid. The poor, poor fool.

As she reached the corner of Second Avenue, she told herself enough was enough. She was sick of getting pushed around. As she headed back to the apartment, she decided it was time to do a little pushing back her own self.

Twenty-Three

*The fact that I'd mistaken him for anything other than a
typical shithead policeman could mean I was disgustingly
superficial, capable of allowing my entire perspective on life
and law enforcement to be swayed by...what?
A smile? A few kind words?*
ALISON GAYLIN, *Hide Your Eyes*

Joe Miscali was having a very bad day. After the complete fuck-up with the drug bust, the freaking SWAT team on Staten Island, the wrong location, and, oh Jesus, the *Daily News*, his fellow cops had been breaking his balls all day, going, "Hey, Joe, you got any hot tips, don't tell us, okay?"

Like that.

And Felicia winding up dead didn't help. Like he was ever gonna get another source when he let his people get wasted, half-eaten by freaking seagulls?

Joe was biting his nails, one of the reasons his wife had legged it. At the marriage counselor's she'd screamed at him, "I'm sick of you and your fucking anxiety!" Christ, if she could see him now.

His phone shrilled and he was seriously thinking of not answering it, one more shitheel taking a shot at him. He picked up anyway, fearing the worst.

It was Rodriguez, one of his undercovers, who'd been tailing Max and Kyle. Rodriguez had been stationed outside Fisher's building for hours. Now he said there was movement. Kyle, the 'Bama boy who palled around with Fisher, had come out of the building and gotten into a cab with some chesty blonde, maybe an UnSub. Miscali started shouting, telling Rodriguez to get his ass in gear and follow them. Rodriguez sounded real hurt, shot back that if Joe thought he wasn't up to the job, yada yada. So now Joe had to, like, placate the guy for, what, five minutes, telling him what a terrific cop he was, with the rest of the Department lapping it up, until Rodriguez calmed down.

Rodriguez called Miscali back later, said he'd tailed Kyle and the broad to Sixth Street, Little India. He said they went into a building together, then the woman came out alone, and then went back in again a minute later.

Rodriguez went to Miscali, "What am I supposed to do?"

"Do?" Miscali shot back. "Stay the fuck where you are is what you do."

He put the phone down, tried to figure out what the hell was going on, who the hell the broad was.

Slide went, "Fook," as he hefted the kid's weight on his shoulder, tried to get the balance right. He thought, Jaysus, this kidnapping lark is fooking hard work is what it is, how come they never show that in the fookin' movies?

And here was the bold Angela, back in the apartment going, "Put him down, now."

Like she was Miss Super Hero, come to save the day.

Raging, Slide dropped the kid onto a chair, going, "I thought I told you to leg it." The kid had a piece of cloth tied in his mouth as a gag and bruises on the side of his face. He was unconscious.

It was hard to read Angela's expression behind the dark shades. She said, "You promised you wouldn't hurt him."

"Gimme a fookin' break," Slide said, "and get me a cold one, the kid is heavier than he looks." Slide tied the kid's arms behind the chair with a length of chain, then wrapped the remainder of the chain around Kyle's chest and legs. Then he got a basin of water and lashed it into the kid's face, going, "Wakey wakey."

"Thank God," Angela said as Kyle's eyes opened. "Slide, listen to me. I want you to let him go."

Slide laughed.

"I'm not joking," Angela said, and she grabbed the butcher knife from where Slide had left it when getting the basin. Pointing the knife at Slide's throat she went, "Let him go."

"The fook're you going to do with that?" he asked.

"I'm not going to get mixed up in another fookin' murder because of you."

"So what're you going to do, kill me? That's a good way not to get involved in another murder—kill somebody."

"I will if I have to."

"Oh, Christ, just put the knife down and give me a hand here. We're wasting valuable time."

"I'll put the knife down when he's safe."

Slide laughed, said, "That's a great plan. You think he'll go home and decide not to tell anyone he was kidnapped? I guess we'll just hope he sees the fun in it, eh?"

"He might not tell," Angela said.

"Oh, stop with that shite talk and give me the knife." Slide reached out, but Angela didn't give it to him.

She said, "I'm not going to let you hurt him."

"Don't you get it?" Slide said. "This is the way it has to be. If we hurt him a little he'll be afraid, then when we release him he'll keep his mouth shut. Trust me— I've studied kidnapping and I know how the gig works. We have to hurt him, but I won't kill him, I promise you that. Now just give me the fookin' knife."

Slide inched closer to Angela then he lunged toward her suddenly and wrested the knife away. They stood looking at each other for a moment, he with the knife, watching his own reflection in the lenses of her glasses. For a moment, they both wondered whether he was going to plunge the knife into her. But he didn't. He swung his other arm around in a roundhouse instead, clocked her solidly on the temple, and she went down like the proverbial steer.

He dragged her out of the way, then got busy, spreading plastic on the floor, especially under the chair where the kid was sitting.

Slide knew he had to cut something off. A finger, an ear, whatever. That's the way it was done. It's how you showed you were serious.

In his chair, the kid was struggling weakly.

"What shall I cut, boy?" Slide grabbed him by the hair, tugged the boy's right ear away from the side of his head. Just like slicing off a chicken wing. *Ear's lookin' at you, kid.* But ears, ears had been done, like, so often, they were fookin' old. He needed something new, something original. Then, bingo, it came to him. Oh, man.

He unbuckled the kid's belt and worked the kid's jeans and Y-fronts down over his hips. The kid was near catatonic with fear.

Slide stepped back to marvel—this kid had a whopper all right.

"Fook, not even the black fellahs could equal that," he said.

He grabbed the dick, and began to cut.

When she came to, Angela heard Kyle whimpering. Slide was nowhere in sight. She went over to Kyle, saw his pants around his knees, saw the crude pressure bandage Slide had put in place, saw the blood all over, and she ran into the bathroom, barely reaching the sink before violently throwing up.

Twenty-Four

He was as attractive as a barracuda.
DESCRIPTION OF ROBERT STROUD,
THE BIRDMAN OF ALCATRAZ

Max knew what he was looking at and it didn't take him long to figure out who it had belonged to. He had once walked in on Kyle taking a leak and had noticed the kid's huge dong. At first he was surprised and—let's face it—jealous, but then he realized it made total sense. Little brain, big dick, right?

Speaking of brains, Max racked his, trying to figure out who could've done this and why. He'd found another note in the box—in addition to the NOW WHO'S A DICK? one—warning that if Max didn't deliver $50,000 in cash to the "phone box" on the corner of Second Avenue and Fourteenth Street by 1:00 PM, more pieces of Kyle would arrive. Yeah, like Max would ever pay a penny to get Kyle back. Shit, Kyle out of the picture helped Max—if the kid was dead Max wouldn't have to worry about him flipping on him for the drug shooting.

But Max still wanted to know who was behind this, if only for his own safety. The one explanation that made any sense to him was that it had to have been the fat guy from the drug deal, what the hell did

Felicia say his name was? Shoe-Shoe? Yeah, Shoe-Shoe must've nabbed Kyle in revenge and cut off his dick, the sick fuck.

Then Max had a thought that horrified him a lot more than the sight of the Ziplocked dick lying on the floor. What if Shoe-Shoe came after Max next? The thought of getting his dick chopped off terrified Max to the point where he was ready to call the cops and get his ass arrested pronto. Spending the rest of his life in jail, or even the death penalty, had to be better than walking around dickless.

But then Max managed to calm himself, his old Zen side taking over. He thought, *Okay, be wise, Maxie, be in the now*. Yeah, Shoe-Shoe was bonkers, but maybe this was it—maybe one dick was enough for him. After all, the note had been, *Now who's a dick?* Not, *Whose dick is coming off next?* This gave Max some reassurance.

Max stared at the dick, nudged the bag with the tip of his shoe. He was mesmerized by its size. For years Max had been using pumps and taking pills trying to enlarge his dick, but to no avail. Max wondered— couldn't those things be transplanted nowadays? If they could do hearts and livers they had to be able to do dicks, right? And didn't that guy down south, Bobbitt, get his reattached after his old lady dumped it on the road? Kyle was from the south—maybe there was something about southern dicks. Maybe Max could go for dick replacement surgery or whatever the hell it was called. Maybe he should, like, save the dick just in case. Hell, what if Shoe-Shoe showed up at the apartment later and chopped off Max's dick? Wouldn't it be good to have a spare?

He entertained the idea for a moment, but the moment passed. He picked up the Ziplock with two fingers, went out to the hallway, and dropped it down the garbage chute.

Slide was seriously antsy. He'd been hanging out at the phone box on Fourteenth and Second since dropping off the package. He was waiting for Fisher, but there was no sign of the bastard. What the fook was with that? You get a dick hand-delivered to your building and you don't even show?

He said aloud, "Bollocks."

He was drinking Coors Light, yeah, *Light*, not by choice, mind, he'd hit a deli and that's what they'd had.

He asked himself, What's with Fisher? Why is he ignoring us? Is he scared to leave his apartment?

And right away, he knew what to do.

He caught a cab, went directly to Fisher's building, and told the doorman he was a police officer, quickly flipped his wallet open and shut. Nothing in there but a MetroCard, but Slide must have made a convincing-looking cop, or could've been the Irish accent, because the guy let him right up.

He took the elevator to the penthouse, rang the buzzer. The door opened slowly and there he was, the man himself, looking a little the worse for wear, like he'd been on a speed jag or some such shite.

Max went, "Yes?"

Slide figured this guy would be a pushover, said, "It's about your young friend."

Fisher looked sick, as if he was going to throw up and then said in a weak voice, "Shoe-shoe sent you."

Slide thought, The fook was Shoe-Shoe? but, going along with it went, "That's right."

Max looked disgusted, as if something had stirred some vile memory, and said, "Jesus Christ, you're not fucking Irish, are you?"

Jaysus, and Slide had thought his American had been coming along so well.

"Actually, I'm of British descent," he said, trying to sound miffed.

"Eh, Irish, British, same bullshit," Fisher said and waved him in.

Slide followed, noticing the package on the counter and wondered where the item was. Must be fairly ripe by now.

Slide decided to play it as it laid, went, "My partner, see, he's a psycho, I tried to stop him from cutting the…you know, but he's impossible to control. He wanted to kill the kid. If he knew I was here, he'd kill me."

Fisher's eyes got a sly sheen and Slide knew the guy was figuring the odds. Fisher said, "You're not exactly tight with your partner, huh?"

Slide nearly laughed but kept it reined, and said, "I won't lie to you, Mr. Fisher, I want the cash but some things, they're just not right and anyway my, um, partner, he'd as soon kill me as share the money."

Fook, he was losing track of who he was supposed

to be, but Fisher helped with, "So, you'd be open to a new deal, one that, let's say, terminated your agreement with Shoe-Shoe?"

Slide had forgotten the name and was delighted to hear it again. He tried to put on a serious look and said, "What is it you're proposing, Mr. Fisher?"

Fisher looked wired now, as if he'd won a new lease on life. He headed for the bar, asked, "Get you something?"

Slide, in a real mood for playing, went, "Got any Coors Light?"

Twenty-Five

Showing a woman your pistol is just like
showing her your cock.
CHARLES WILLEFORD, *New Hope for the Dead*

Angela, still wearing her shades, took a deep gulp of vodka. She'd discovered a bottle of Stoli in Slide's stuff—rifling through his gear was habitual now—and, hello, she'd also found a Browning automatic. She didn't actually know it was a Browning but she sure as shit knew what it felt like—reassurance in her hand. When you had a piece in your hand you knew no one would be fucking with you, least not twice.

Notwithstanding her horrendous year in Dublin, Angela was still prone to all the superstitions that the Irish half of her heritage had bestowed. She checked in her purse and sure enough, there was the gold pin of two hands nearly touching—her lucky charm. The evidence of her life would contradict the notion that the pin had brought her much in the way of luck lately, but hey, the way she was feeling she'd have stuck pins in a friggin doll if it might help. She attached the pin above her bust and the light caught the tiny hint of gold. It gave her a moment if not of peace, then of resolve.

She took a breath and walked out to where Kyle sat. His moans had been ferocious for the hour he'd been conscious.

The gun was in her hand, hanging casually along-side her hip. The kid's face was contorted. Angela peered over the top of her shades at him. Jesus, what a poor bastard. She felt her heart melt.

His eyes opened and he looked at her.

Jesus, she thought. Sweet bloody Jesus. The things we do.

She touched the gun to his forehead, between his eyes. He closed his eyes. She'd been hoping for a nod, but fuck it, you take the signs you get. She intoned, *Jesus, Mary and Joseph, forgive me for I do know what I'm about to do, have to do.*

She pulled the trigger. The recoil from the gun knocked her back. A spray of blood spattered against the plastic.

Then she threw up again. She went back for the Stoli and lots of it, the gun still in her hand. She wasn't letting go of that baby—it was all she had.

She went into the tiny bedroom, threw some things in a suitcase, then came back to the chair. Was it mad-ness or did the dumb-arse kid look...peaceful? She leant over and took the pin from her bust, put it on the kid's bloodstained shirt. The gold seemed to have dulled, and the hands were further away from touching than ever. Then, without a backward glance, she opened the door, and didn't bang it, just let it close softly. Joyce would have been proud of her. What he would have made of the Browning in her case is any-body's guess.

*

Sha-Sha was in Canarsie, corner of 102nd and L, having his ass a little snack—couple dozen White Castle cheeseburgers. He was eating 'em two at a time, washing them with soda—Diet Coke cause he was trying to lose some weight—when he saw the white man coming toward him. Nigga wasn't no customer—must be a damn cop. But that disguise, man, it wasn't working. Mother-fucker tryin' too hard to look undercover, with them shades and the hair and the beard and shit.

Sha-Sha been through this po-lice bullshit a million times before. He made like he was just minding his own, chompin' on the White Castles, acting like he didn't give a shit.

The man went up to him and said, "You'll be Sha-Sha?"

He had this fucked-up accent, like the nigga was trying to sound like damn U2.

"The fuck wants to know?" Sha-Sha asked. He gulped down some soda, tossed the can on the street, like he was sayin', *You can bust my ass for litterin' you want, but that's all you gonna get, nigga.*

But then the Bono dude went, "Answer my fookin' question. Is your name Sha-Sha?"

Sick of playing this bullshit, Sha-Sha went, "Yeah, I'm Sha-Sha, now how 'bout you get the fuck out my face, punk?"

Sha-Sha looked away and spat. When he looked back the dude was holding some big-ass knife, looked like you could carve up a turkey with it. Sha-Sha was thinking, *The fuck kind of cop is this?*

Slide had partied hard with Max at the penthouse, doing coke, pot, vodka, even shared a few hits on his crack pipe. It was some good shite and Max—sorry, *The M.A.X.*—was a great guy, first person in eons Slide didn't want to off. Slide felt like he and Max seriously connected. They both loved American film, especially anything with De Niro or Pacino. And, besides, how could he kill a guy who did a pretty good Brit accent his own self?

Max, high as a kite, had told him about some woman, Felicia, who'd screwed him over by selling him out to her 500-pound cousin Shoe-Shoe who lived in Canarsie. Slide was relieved because he'd had no idea how he'd find this fookin Shoe-Shoe guy, but when Max gave him the bit of info he figured, How many Shoe-Shoes could there be in Canarsie? Wherever fookin Canarsie was.

Max told Slide he would pay him one hundred thousand dollars in cash if Slide took care of Shoe-Shoe for him. Slide couldn't believe this deal—he was actually going to get paid to kill someone? That was like telling a guy who sat around jerking off all day, watching pornos, that he would now receive hard cash every time he ejaculated. Slide wanted to pinch himself.

An hour later, he left Max's, found this Canarsie place on a subway map, and headed out to Brooklyn, to Shoe-Shoe's—what was the term the brothers used?— oh yeah, *hood*.

Off the L train, he asked the first drug dealer he

spotted if he knew where he could find a dealer named Shoe-Shoe who weighed about five hundred pounds. No luck there or with the next couple lowlife-looking types. But then he found a skinny, nervous guy outside a schoolyard who seemed to have the info. The fellah wasn't exactly forthcoming, but Slide persuaded him to open up by placing his knife to the fook's throat.

The guy spilled. "His name ain't Shoe-Shoe, man, it's Sha-Sha. He's up on his corner, Hundred and Second an' L. Please don't kill me, man. Please don't—"

Slide stabbed him in the chest. Straight to the heart —in, out, wipe. Would've had some more fun with him but Slide was in a hurry and had, like, important business to take care of.

Then Slide found Sha-Sha. How could he miss him? The bollix was the size of a small car. His mouth was stuffed with food—big surprise there—and Slide went to him, "You'll be Sha-Sha?"

The guy gave him some mouth about who wants to know, and some other shite talk, and then Slide revealed the blade. He didn't have the reaction Slide expected. Yeah, there was terror in his eyes, but he didn't start begging and screaming the way most victims did. He'd probably had machetes, hooks, broken bottles, you name it, put up to him and he did the very worst thing he could've done—he waved Slide away, like he was some minor irritation.

This pissed Slide off to no end. Didn't the fat fook know who he was dealing with? For a moment, Slide nearly leaned over and gutted him there and then, but he chilled, as his new buddy, The M.A.X., was fond of saying. Instead, he grabbed one of the burgers, took a healthy bite, chewed down, said, "Needs a little more ketchup, don't you think?"

Now he had the guy's attention. Yeah, the guy's mouth was hanging open, like he couldn't believe this skinny fellah had taken his food. It was like Sha-Sha had seen all kinds of stuff in his career but the one line you did not cross, ever, was to fuck with his food.

His mouth still full, he'd gurgled something like, "De fu…c…de…ddddoin?"

Slide wondered if the guy was rapping. He knew these dudes rapped on just about everything.

To get him focused, Slide took a nice swipe out of his cheek, just one fast stroke of the blade and there, a nice tribal scar for him. Weren't these guys into all kinds of colors and markings, or was that Indians? What the fook ever.

Slide gave him his best smile—now the guy was all attention—and said, "I like black dudes, really I do. Phil Lynott, now there was one cool cat, you dig? And for a moment there, I was going to let this slide, just mosey on my way, let you finish this little feast you were at, but you know, you gave me cheek." Slide laughed. "Cheek, sorry, I'm a mick, punning is our gig." Then he put the knife in Sha-Sha's throat with maximum force. The knife was so deeply imbedded that it took Slide a few moments to extract it, and he muttered, "Dunno me own strength."

Sha-Sha's knees buckled and he fell onto the sidewalk. He squirmed for a few seconds, belched a few times, then he wasn't moving no more.

Slide reached down, popped a bite of burger in his mouth, thinking, you could develop a taste for those suckers. He stared at the enormous body on the ground for a moment, thinking, *Trophy?*

He bent down, pulled off one of Sha-Sha's sneakers, stared at it, went, "Got your Shoe-Shoe, Sha-Sha."

He loved that, repeated it to himself all the way back to the city.

About an hour later, back in Manhattan, Slide gave The M.A.X. the sneaker and along with it, the rundown on Sha-Sha's last meal.

"Son of a bitch," Max said, "you really did it." Then he said to the sneaker, in his hip-hop voice, "You be de shoo-in, baby," and tossed it away over his shoulder.

He and Slide cracked up over this—were these guys on the same page or what?

They had a few brews, just two buddies, sinking a few. From time to time they looked over at the sneaker in the corner and toasted to it.

Finally, Slide, much fun as this was, said, "I gotta, like, get moving, so if you can give me the cash, I'll be on me way."

Max suddenly looked pained and Slide hoped he wasn't going to start fucking around. He would really not want to have to gut the likable bastard.

Max raised his hands, let them fall. "I'm broke. I have, tops, eight or nine grand. I might be able to raise more later but right now, that's it."

Whacked out, Max found this amusing, started giggling.

Slide surprised himself, said, "Let's see it."

Max led Slide to the bedroom closet. He opened the safe and took out the wads of bills and Slide, an edge in his tone now, said, "Count it."

Max did. There was nine grand and change.

Slide snatched the cash from Max's hand, stuffed it in his pocket. Max whined, "C'mon, can't you leave me a few bucks for, you know, necessities?"

Slide gave him back two singles, said, "Knock yourself out."

Max didn't argue.

When Slide reached the door, Max said, "I guess this is *adios*, *muchacho*?"

Slide lunged, as if he was going to stab Max in the gut, and Max jerked back. But, alas, Slide wasn't holding the knife.

"Nope, not *adios* for you yet," Slide said, smiling. "Not if you can round up the rest of my money in, say, two days. Nah, let's make it one."

"But I can't—"

"Sh," Slide said. "Don't say can't. Don't say won't. Say yes I will." He patted Max on the side of the face. "I'll be back."

Slide cabbed it back to the apartment on Sixth Street. He was tired, in need of a bit of grub, maybe a quick violent shag from Angela, and then he was going to have him some serious z's.

But the minute he entered the apartment, he knew something was up.

There was no sign of Angela, no screaming and moaning from the kid. Then he saw Kyle's body, the bullet hole in his forehead. So she'd taken the kid out—fook, Slide was impressed.

This Angela and Max, they were some pair all right. Slide had never come across the likes of them, and he wasn't sure he wanted to again. They had their good qualities, but they were a little too out there, even for him. They were always doing weird shite. It was kind of spooky actually, gave Slide the creeps. He needed to be among ordinary folk, the type you could kill and they didn't screw around, didn't make any big fuss, just took their licks and didn't do anything.

He went to the dresser, packed a few shirts, noticed Angela had taken his Browning. He said, "Mad fooker."

Outside, he was leaving the apartment when a guy approached him and Slide thought, *Cop*.

Sure enough, the guy introduced himself, went, "Rodriguez, NYPD."

The guy was polite enough, wanted to know if Slide had seen a young kid, blond hair, maybe with a woman —blond, sunglasses, a nice shape.

Slide gave him his best smile and his best New York accent, said, "No, sir, and let me say, I sure admire you for the work you do, can't be easy."

Slide started to walk away when the guy said, "Excuse me, sir," and Slide knew this was trouble.

"Yep," Slide said calmly.

"I had a talk before with the woman who manages the restaurant above your apartment," Rodriguez said, "and she said she thought she heard some strange noises coming from there earlier, sounded like someone screaming."

"How do you know it's my flat?"

"Because I watched you go in a little while ago."

Yep, this was trouble, but Slide was looking forward to it. Doing guards always gave him a rush.

"I'm just fookin' with you," Slide said. "It's my flat but there's no kid and no woman in there. Want to take a look inside?"

"If you don't mind," Rodriguez said.

Slide led Rodriguez into the building. In the vestibule, Slide fumbled in his coat pocket, going, "My fookin' key, where is it?" Meanwhile, he was opening the five-inch switchblade he kept in the inside pocket.

Slide turned, ready to slash the cop's throat, when the fook fired his gun and Slide felt pain rip though his side. He was coming again with the blade but the Rodriguez bastard fired again and Slide slid down against the door, till he was seated on the floor, his ass soaking in his own blood. Shite, this was no way for a serial killer to go down. He hadn't even come close to any of the records.

He was looking up at Rodriguez, then everything turned foggy. The cop's face turned into Angela's—the mad cow looking down at Slide, and was she fookin laughing?

Slide was trying to mumble something so Rodriguez leant down, trying to catch it.

Slide gasped, "Was…gonna …let…it…slide."

The cop said, "You lied? You lied about what?"

Slide tried again.

"Yeah, fucking scumbags like you always lie," the cop said.

A gurgle in Slide's throat, and he was history.

Twenty-Six

I am the wickedest man in New York.
THEODORE "THE ALIEN" ALLEN, GANGSTER

When Joe Miscali broke down the door to Max's apartment and entered with a whole goddamn SWAT team Max knew this wouldn't be the usual bust.

Couple of cops pushed Max face-down onto the carpet and cuffed him and Max whined, "Ow, you're hurting me."

Max wondered what the hell had happened to his machismo? It abandoned him at a time like this, when he needed it most? Jesus H.

"You cocksucker," Miscali said. "You thought you could fuck me over, you son of a bitch. You little piece of shit."

"What are you gonna arrest me for?" Max said. "You can't prove anything."

"You think you're so fuckin' smart, you're a fuckin' brain surgeon now, huh?" Miscali said. "For possession of whatever shit we find in the apartment...and, oh, yeah, and for murder."

"I didn't shoot that fuckin' gang kid," Max said.

"I'm not talking about that murder," Miscali said, "though don't think you're not gonna go down for that too. I'm talking about the murder of Kyle Jordan."

"Hey, I had nothing to do with that shit," Max said. "Honest."

"If you didn't kill Jordan," Miscali said. "How come we just recovered his penis in your garbage room? You wanna tell me that?"

"His penis?" Max said. "I never saw that penis before in my life."

"And how about the blonde with the big tits?" Miscali said. "You're gonna tell me you haven't been in contact with Angela Petrakos?"

Max started to smile, thought, *So it* was *her. Son of a bitch.*

"Answer my goddamn questions," Miscali said.

"As far as I know, Angela isn't even in this country," Max said.

"My guy saw her pick up Kyle Jordan in front of your apartment."

"How do you know it was her?"

Miscali showed Max a gold pin. Shit, it was the one Angela used to wear, of two hands almost touching.

"My buddy Kenneth Simmons had this pin because his son had Down Syndrome," Miscali said. "Then after Simmons was killed you somehow got hold of the pin and gave it to Angela Petrakos. That was the theory anyway. Now the same pin winds up on the body of Kyle Jordan. You wanna explain that to me?"

Max, with tears in his eyes—hey, he was a sentimental guy—said, "Wow, the pin. I never thought I'd see that pin again. Can I just, like, touch it?"

Miscali, looking like he was about to lose it big time, roared, "Get this cocksucker out of my sight!"

The cops led Max away in handcuffs. He was still confused about a lot of things, especially why in God's name Angela had chopped off Kyle's dick and then killed him, but he focused on the important thing—she was alive; she was out there somewhere.

Leaving the building, Max didn't know what was going on, said, "Whoa, what's going on?"

Where were the crowds? Where was the media? Didn't the whole city want to, like, come out to see The M.A.X. take his fall?

Eh, the President was probably in town, or maybe it was Super Sunday or Christmas Day. Yeah, it had to be something big like that.

As they stuffed Max into the back of the police car, Max smiled in a cocky way, like John Gotti did whenever he got sent away. It was like Max was telling the cops, *Maybe you got me this time, but I'll live to fight another day.*

Yeah, The M.A.X. knew that, no matter what, he was looking at some time here, but he was getting into the idea. He was a big-time criminal now, a pro, and pros always had to do a stretch or two during the course of their careers. It was part of the biz; it came with the territory. And, hell, it was better than rehab. Yeah, he knew he'd have a blast behind bars. Celebs like him always got protection from the thugs and women went nuts for notorious prisoners. He'd begin a proper study of Zen, become a master, maybe even bop over to India when he got out, to finesse his calling. And did any-one understand the law better than The M.A.X.? He'd be like Jimmy Woods in *The Onion Field*—the elder statesman, still with a fucking dangerous mind but, you know, not showy with it. Oh, and inside you know he was going to be flooded with love letters and marriage proposals from an assortment of babes. Naturally, Angela would write to him. She'd say how lonely she was and how she was counting the days till his release. Maybe she'd even show up to visit, bring him cakes, and then when his parole came through she'd be waiting for him in a red Porsche. Ah, then he'd have the HBO series, the *Wall Street Journal* column, and everything else he'd ever wanted.

The cop car pulled away and The M.A.X., in the back seat, was grinning his fucking ass off.

The driver looked up at Max in the rearview, smiled, and the other cop next to him, chewing on gum, said something and they both laughed together.

The M.A.X. didn't hear what they were saying but he knew, like all knowledge that had been given to him, that they were trying to decide which of them would ask him for his autograph. He fingered his hair—hell, he was feeling expansive, he might even give them a lock of it, let them sell it on eBay, bring some bucks into their mundane fucking lives.

He thought, *Whoops, I cursed, gonna have to give that up.*

He wondered if he should ask them to put on the sirens, let the little people know a player was en route.

But then he decided to ride with the humility gig, no need to be flashy. As the mad Brit had told him while they were freebasing—sometimes you just gotta let it slide.